Gort

Gort

Gary W. Roberto

To order additional copies of this book, contact:
Xlibris Corporation
1-888-795-4274
www.Xlibris.com
Orders@Xlibris.com
77051

Contents

Introduction

There have been many strange theories narrated concerning the destruction and desolation of our once-vibrant planet. There are very few of us alive today who know the full and true story of what really happened and, more importantly, why it happened. I am one of those few.

My name is Robert Benson. I am an astrophysicist. I am also a quantum mechanics physicist and professor. In the summer of 1951, I was nine years old when I first met Mr. Carpenter, and I immediately became fascinated by this tall, thin stranger who came to stay at the boarding house where my mother and I lived. In fact, he quickly became my best friend. However, he did not come to visit our planet alone on that fateful day. And I must say, I still tend to tremble with fear when I remember the robot he brought with him. My mother, Helen, a widow at that time as my father had died in World War II, may have come to know Mr. Carpenter a bit more intimately than I. The particular part her relationship with Mr. Carpenter played in saving our world cannot be understated or minimized. And I can derive some small source of pleasure by stating I was there at the beginning and am also able, by the grace of the Almighty Spirit, to be here at the end. I am now seventy years old, and as does seem to be the case at times, with age comes a certain amount of wisdom.

It is perhaps due to this wisdom or experience that I found myself working with the United States Air Force in an advisory capacity. I definitely considered myself quite fortunate to be stationed at the Cheyenne Mountain Complex, just outside of Colorado Springs, Colorado. I had completed some work for the U.S. government in the past and as a result had obtained a *most secret* security clearance. As a result of this and other factors too numerous to mention, I had accepted the rather elite invitation to be part of the team at the complex. As with most military commands, I found it to be populated by extremely dedicated, energetic, and diligent personnel. These, undoubtedly, were some of our nation's best.

It was with a certain amount of pleasure and satisfaction that I found myself at level 5 of the Cheyenne Mountain Complex. Every day turned out to be an extremely interesting day, for the complex is the site of some of the most technological wonders of the world. This center houses numerous computers, processors, displays, and communication links, which coordinate and control NORAD (North American Aerospace Defense Command). Within the Cheyenne Mountain Complex are various centers that conduct missile, atmospheric, and space warning activities. The Air Operations Center (AOC) is in constant motion maintaining strict surveillance of the North American airspace, while the Missile Warning Center (MWC) works to detect any launch of a missile globally. The center's personnel then work diligently to determine the missile's ultimate threat capabilities. The Space Control Center (SCC), or otherwise known as the Space Defense Operations Center (SPADOC) detects, identifies, and immediately begins tracking any man-made object in space. They have the unenviable task of maintaining constant and continuous tracking of thousands of objects in space, affectionately known as space junk. The NORAD Command Center (NCC) functions as the core for any and all activities within the complex. This is where the command director, usually a brigadier general, performs his duty twenty-four hours a day.

His second in command, the executive officer, is usually a full bird colonel who commands the complex in the absence of the general. Each has had their turn commanding this complex, which provides for the coordination and direction to all the different sections within the command. If the need arises, the command director can be in communication with the president of the United States and the prime minister of Canada within a few seconds. This center also supports the commander in chief NORAD to provide warning and attack assessment on North America or its allies. Also housed in the Cheyenne Mountain Complex is the Combined Intelligence Center (CIC), which serves as the advanced warning center for possible attacks from space or other threats from any air/space activity. CIC operational mission is to quickly gather intelligence information, and then to rapidly assist all Cheyenne Mountain work centers in correlating and analyzing events as they unfold, immediately reporting their findings to the U.S. Space command decision makers.

I was there in the Combined Intelligence Center at the Cheyenne Mountain Complex outside of Colorado Springs, Colorado, when these astounding events began to unfold with frightful velocity. As history now records, the pace of events of that horrific time did not slacken, did not offer even a moment of respite, from the terrible tragedies to be played out on the world stage.

This, then, is the only true account of the events and subsequent proceedings, which seem almost inaccessible to ordinary understanding. This will be all I have to say of these unfortunate events, and I will decline any further conversation upon the subject.

Chapter One

Arrival

0245 hrs
21 Dec 2012
U.S. Space Command
Cheyenne Mountain Complex

A pair of eyes peered intently through the dimly lit interior of the subterranean structure. The main focus of their rapt attention was the large computer console screen directly in front of them. The eyes, belonging to air force Staff Sergeant Larry Lessard, suddenly opened wide in astonishment. The screen, abruptly and contrary to all reasonable expectation, lit up like a Christmas tree as an unidentified object appeared clearly halfway across the monitor. In another second, the ghostly image had disappeared entirely. I, through a timely bit of sheer coincidence, had been standing behind and to the left of his station, alternately observing his monitor and that of "the big screen" occupying a large section of wall some twenty feet in front of me.

"Doc? Did you see that?" Lessard stammered in openmouthed astonishment as he abruptly turned toward me. His voice betrayed a sense of curiosity crossed with utter bewilderment.

"Affirmative," I replied in my best representation of a military voice. Although I had spent four years of my life in the United States Marine Corps upon turning eighteen years old those many years ago, I had never forgotten the armed forces lingo that had been imprinted upon my psyche. After all, "Once a Marine, always a Marine." So as a direct consequence, once in a while I tried to join in conversations in a military manner. All at times of my own choosing, of course.

"Guess you better call the captain in on this, Larry," I responded with scarcely a second thought. I must admit the unexpected development had not yet fully stimulated my curiosity.

"Captain?" the voice of the staff sergeant called out. Lessard, a droll fellow in a sardonic way, possessed red curly hair and a clean-cut face. He stood roughly six feet in height and, like most military personnel at this base, was in excellent physical condition. Cognizant of his duty, Lessard was to immediately report all anomalies of any kind to his immediate superior. And to the sergeant, who in his one and a half years of duty at this station had never in all his past experience at the complex ever observed even the slightest irregularity, this momentary anomaly certainly qualified as unusual. I could hear the captain ascend from his chair and begin the slow, measured walk toward Lessard's station. Resuming his intent scrutiny of the screen, Larry continued speaking with me while the captain made his way over to his station. "Either my equipment just experienced some sort of malfunction, or something just crossed my screen traveling at an excessive . . . an incredible speed! This object must have been approaching the speed of light! You know, Doc, maybe this is the beginning of that 2012 stuff you've been talking about. You know . . . the Earth, the Sun aligned with the center of the universe, the end of the Mayan calendar, and all the Nostradamus predictions."

I moved in for a closer look, and I do not hesitate to confess that a nervous restlessness was now beginning to make its way up the back of my spine. What I had inadvertently witnessed was now beginning to cause me some concern and anxiety.

"Video playback please, Sergeant," replied the calm and assertive voice of captain John Meyers. The captain had come close enough to hear the sergeant's last remarks. "Let's not hurry into miscalculation, shall we?"

Captain Meyers, who now stood directly behind Lessard, was a graduate of the Air Force Academy with seven years' service. As such, he was not an individual prone to excitement and insisted everything be done by the book. Meyers was a tall young man of about twenty-eight years of age, with thick black and neatly cropped, military-style hair, and a slightly hooked nose. His father, James Meyers, had retired an air force general, and John Meyers was bound and determined to accomplish the same feat. To Captain Meyers, it was of supreme importance he attain the same type of career his father had managed to achieve. Before his retirement, the captain's father had helped to arrange this assignment at the Cheyenne Mountain Complex. John Meyers was more than aware this was a highly coveted position. He was determined not to screw anything up, so by the book he went. Captain Meyers had summarily positioned himself behind Lessard to observe the video playback, which was now starting to flash across the screen.

After the blip on the screen appeared and disappeared in astonishing rapidity, the staff sergeant's eyes finally deserted their post and looked up toward the captain.

"Well, sir, what do you think?" asked Lessard.

The captain, who was known to be among the calmest thinkers within the complex, took a couple of seconds to gather his thoughts. Like the sergeant, during his time on station, he had not observed any event of a similar nature. Unable to contain my curiosity any longer, my eyes finally moved from the computer screen to the captain's face as well. There had been a short, but distinct pause as he considered the available options.

"Larry, has your equipment been giving you any problems recently?" asked the captain in a calm, cool voice.

"No, sir. All equipment was functioning within normal parameters."

"I see," responded the captain with more than a noticeable consternation apparent in his voice. "All right then, run a level 1 diagnostic check on everything, will you? Just to be sure."

"Yes, sir," replied Lessard, who immediately returned his attention to the computer.

"Janet!" the captain said with a raised voice so as to be heard over the clatter of the many machines within the structure. I listened intently and with much curiosity as to how the captain had decided to proceed.

Air force tech sergeant Janet Huckabee, the level 5 communications and control noncommissioned officer, had been watching the proceedings from her desk of operations a few steps behind and to the right. She had been doing so with more than just idle curiosity. Janet was really quite striking in her beauty as she had perfectly chiseled features and Nordic blonde hair. Being from Atlanta, Georgia, she spoke with an intoxicating Southern drawl. She possessed a charming and infectious enthusiasm as well. She knew very well that through the command's global positioning system, the defense satellite communications system phase III, and the NATO V communications and fleet satellite system, the U.S. Space Command center would know with absolute certainty where all known satellites and spacecraft are located at any given time. That something was not where it was supposed to be, or that something new had appeared within the Air Force Satellite Control Network, was more than just a mystery, it was damn near impossible. My feeling of uneasiness was rapidly beginning to escalate.

"Yes, sir?" she replied with raised anticipation. Her gaze was steady and cold.

"Ring up the colonel for me, would you? Ask her to come down here for a moment. I think we may need her," answered Captain Meyers in a relatively calm and collected voice, as he once again resumed his intent gaze at the screen. This was not an abrupt decision but was borne out of careful consideration and conscientious calculations. The captain turned his attention back to Sergeant Lessard. He gently rested his hand upon Lessard's shoulder and spoke.

"Let's not get carried away with the end-of-the-world-as-we-know-it scenario just yet, shall we, Larry?" continued the captain with a shade of reproach in his voice.

"No, sir," replied Lessard with a slight shrug of his shoulders. "Mighty peculiar though . . ."

A moment later, tech sergeant Huckabee's Southern accent filled the air once again. Her tone was measured and her voice steady with deliberation.

"I got ahold of Colonel Hatch. She states she is on her way, Captain. She should be here momentarily."

"Thank you, Janet," responded Meyers succinctly. "Also, would you please alert NORAD (North American Aerospace Defense) command that we may have some pertinent information for them momentarily. Might as well cover all the bases on this one."

"Yes, sir," came the automatic response from the communications chief. "Notifying NORAD as we speak."

It was only then I afforded myself a quick glance around the area. I could begin to see activity was starting to pick up within all the separate nerve centers located on level 5. Although a nervous excitement began to ripple throughout the center, it was not exactly unusual for an increased activity event like this to happen at CIC. Almost on a daily basis, for brief intervals of time, a flurry of intense activity would temporarily occur. However, I do not hesitate to confess that in this instance, something felt dreadfully different. Perhaps it was the December 21 date, which brought a surprising foreboding to my mind. I shook my head slightly in an attempt to clear it of such dark thoughts and quickly returned my attention to the screen in front of me. I confess the involuntary gesture was an almost obvious, transparent effort to avoid any discomforting thoughts, and I sheepishly hoped no one had noticed. As I watched with elevated interest, Lessard worked quickly on finishing his diagnostic check on the equipment. As I shifted around nervously, I could feel the captain pressing close again.

"How about that diagnostic, Larry?" asked Captain Meyers with an increasing sense of urgency. It seemed as though the usually unflappable captain was beginning to get caught up in the moment.

"Readings are coming in now, Captain. Computer diagnostics indicate the equipment is functioning within acceptable parameters. Nothing unusual or out of the ordinary to report, sir," stated Staff Sergeant Lessard, as his thin lips compressed for a moment. "At this point I'm not sure what we saw, but whatever it was . . ."

"Attention on deck!" a voice called out from somewhere close by.

"Captain, good morning," came a measured voice, which also was loud, strong, and definite. It was the voice of Colonel Alicia Hatch, the on-duty command officer for level 5. Alicia Hatch was a little woman of about five foot five inches, with a long aquiline nose, and a tight little mouth. She wore egg-shaped glasses and was quite famous within the command for her steady and discerning gaze. She exuded the strong quality of being someone not to be trifled with, and her very well-toned body seemed to back up the statement even more. Colonel Hatch had entered the immediate area a bit more rapidly than originally expected. This was just as well, as the pace of events would soon demand increased attention. The captain, startled only momentarily by the colonel's quick entrance upon the scene, spoke in a calm voice as he turned to face Colonel Hatch.

"Good morning, Colonel. Sorry to have to bring you down here at such an hour, but we—"

"Captain!" the excited voice of Sergeant Larry Lessard cut in with an increased measure of urgency. He leaned toward the computer screen in bewildered agitation. "It just popped up on my screen again! Initial computer assessments indicate a traveling velocity approaching the speed of light! The unknown object's point of origin appears to be from a point in deep space . . . an unknown point . . . somewhere toward the center of the universe."

"I want a full spectrum analysis," Colonel Hatch cut in, "and I want it now or sooner, Sergeant. Captain, please alert Space Defense Operations Center 4. I want them brought in on this. Also, please transmit the coordinates of the anomaly. Let's also get some real-time video processing on this. I want an immediate, crystal-clear view at what we are dealing with. And, Captain? I think we had better contact the Joint Space Operations Center and order for immediate execution a GEODSS (Ground-Based Electro-optical Deep Space Surveillance) sweep toward the target area. Level 1 priority on this."

"I'm on it, Colonel!" answered the captain as he walked quickly away to carry out her orders.

The Ground-Based Electro-Optical Deep Space Surveillance performs its vital mission of tracking all deep space objects by use of its one-meter telescope, which is equipped with the most technologically updated digital camera known as Deep Stare. There are three distinct and separate operational GEODSS sites: Socorro, New Mexico; Diego Garcia, British Indian Ocean Territory; and Maui, Hawaii. Each location has a total of three Deep Stare telescopes that can be focused separately or in conjunction with one another. These electronic telescopes can see an object ten thousand times dimmer than the human eye can detect.

"Colonel Hatch! The unidentified object has just made a course correction of roughly 45 degrees. This change in trajectory now has the object headed straight into our solar system!" exclaimed the staff sergeant in a breathless, high-pitched voice. A kind of mindless disbelief shook me as I stared intently at the screen. Lessard continued with his startling report, "So much for this being some type of natural phenomenon! I can't believe how fast this thing is traveling. Early spectro-analysis reports indicate some sort of metal alloy structure that is of unknown type and origin."

"Oh my god . . ." the words escaped my mouth before I could stop them. I shivered involuntarily as I stood there as still as if I was made of stone. I had originally believed my utterance to be scarcely perceptible, but the colonel heard them. I could sense the colonel moving closer to where I stood. I at once felt embarrassed by the outburst.

"Anything you care to share with the rest of us, Dr. Benson?" she asked as she now stood next to me.

"I have a bad feeling about this," I answered without trying to cover the growing fear within myself.

"Anything a bit more along the lines of scientific analysis would certainly be preferable," she replied with some slight amusement, which was quite noticeable in her voice. Colonel Hatch rarely permitted her sense of humor to come through during duty hours, so I was initially stunned by her comment. I recovered my wits as rapidly as I could and answered back.

"I apologize for my rather easily excitable temperament, but I had a multitude of terrifying thoughts cascading through my mind. I'm afraid most of it was related to an event in my past that I am obliged not to discuss with anyone for fear of my sanity being questioned. Perhaps, Colonel, we could have MISTY 2 and MISTY 3 focus their photographic equipment on the object as well?"

"Very well, Doctor. Finally, an excellent suggestion. Let's see what they can show us. Captain Meyers, please order MISTY 2 and 3 to be brought on line. Hopefully, we should have some video in the next few minutes," she said to no one in particular as she momentarily walked off toward another area of the complex. Apparently, the colonel's attention had now been distracted by some other event occurring within the room.

MISTY 2 and MISTY 3 are two stealth reconnaissance imaging spacecrafts in a continuous orbit at an approximate altitude of 811 kilometers above the surface of the Earth. Their earlier predecessor, MISTY 1 had suddenly vanished in early November 1990, amid constant and considerable speculation as to its fate. It was, however, found spinning erratically in deep space quite by accident in 1997 by a completely astonished astronomer. Although MISTY 2 and MISTY 3 have imagery telescopes in varying shortness of barrels to provide wider views, both have the primary mission of monitoring events on Earth. It would only take the slightest of electronic commands to turn its photographic imagery attention toward the coordinates of the unidentified object in deep space. The inconceivable speed of the object and the course correction it unexpectedly initiated had further enforced my belief that it was now imperative to bring these imaging systems on line.

"Colonel!" shouted Staff Sergeant Lessard excitedly. The colonel abruptly returned to the area and focused her attention on the screen. "We are beginning to receive some photographic images from our deep space surveillance satellites. Full spectrum analysis will be forthcoming shortly from all of our integration intelligence and surveillance systems."

An infinite profusion of thoughts began to cascade through my mind as I took a few unsteady steps over to the screen. I got there just ahead of the colonel and the captain. As I peered at the screen, the first available images seem to be nothing more than an intense brilliancy emanating from the darkness of space.

"Can we increase screen magnification, Sergeant?" asked Captain Meyers urgently.

"Increasing magnification," responded Lessard.

The images soon began to slowly transform themselves into a brilliant light, which seemed to brighten and dim in some sort of a rhythmic pattern. Everyone around the computer console maintained a dead silence as the pictures began to unfold upon the screen. Each succeeding image definitely began to display an improved clarity as the object drew nearer to the region of space our satellites found themselves focusing upon. I scarcely managed to breathe as the object's image slowly evolved and materialized before our eyes. The unidentified object began to assume a cylindrical shape at first then started to alter or transform as the images crystallized upon the screen. I could barely manage to remain standing. A ravening terror began to shake me to my core. As I tried to quiet the growing terror within me, I found myself tensely watching the image on the screen in openmouthed astonishment. As the image crystallized, it became increasingly evident the unknown object . . . was saucer-shaped!

A thousand memories instantly came flooding back to my mind. These images from deep in my past, so horrible, so very terrifying, caused me to freeze in my tracks. I suddenly became aware I was breathing in gasps. I wanted to scream or faint, but yet I refrained and kept still. I could have sworn that everyone in the Cheyenne Complex could hear my labored breathing.

Then, with an alarming velocity, appearing on the photographs was a brilliant, dazzling explosion of white light radiating outward from the saucer-shaped object. The intense light seemed to slowly evolve into overlapping ellipses as it progressed, growing larger over the continuing images, until it fully occupied the entire screen. Then, in a flare of blinding light, the photographic stream of images abruptly ceased! I rubbed my eyes in disbelief, as if to erase the previous startling images from my mind. The more I processed and judged what had just transpired, the more convinced I became these were unmistakable signs of an absolute assault. It was my belief we had just witnessed the first signs of an attack against our planet. The extent of the shock rippled throughout the complex. The profound silence gripping the room was broken by Captain Meyers.

"What the hell just happened, Lessard?"

"I don't know. Might be a malfunction of some sort in the relay circuits, sir," responded the staff sergeant halfheartedly as he began an attempt to adjust for the perceived computer glitch. "I am not receiving any information at all from our deep space surveillance satellite."

"All right, Sergeant," interrupted the colonel, "let's worry about that later. Right now, I want you to activate MISTY 2 and 3 and get their imaging equipment locked on to the object. I want more images now, Sergeant. After we regain our capacity to start receiving more images from our other deep space sources and things begin to calm down, you can then attempt to reestablish contact with the satellite. Captain"—the colonel turned abruptly toward Captain Meyers. There was a tone of anxiety in her voice that was hard to conceal. "Open communications to the ISS (International Space Station) and have them turn the orbiter boom sensor and imaging systems toward the last known position of the unidentified object. I want this object accurately tracked. It is also extremely imperative we have as many photographic systems as we can get on this object. I want to know what we are dealing with, and I mean in no uncertain terms. And, Captain? Let's contact the commanding officer of the facility. Wake him up and get him down here ASAP."

"Very well, Colonel," replied the captain as he quickly strode off to carry out the colonel's orders. After I watched the captain move away from the immediate vicinity in a rather rapid pace, I turned my attention back to Colonel Hatch. I could now perceive some very real concern in her countenance. She continued to stare at the screen with hard, cynical eyes. Her eyes remained fixed and motionless. The voices within the complex had suddenly dropped to a disquieting murmur. I glanced nervously about as I cautiously approached her.

"Colonel," I began as I felt the nervous restlessness run throughout my body. I tried desperately to suppress the shudder that was coursing through me but failed miserably. I quieted my voice until it was almost a whisper. "The loss of the satellite's images does not seem to me to be an event caused by technical difficulties. I believe our satellite has been deliberately attacked and destroyed. And it is painfully obvious to me that this unknown object is the thing that attacked and destroyed it. I suggest we initiate—"

"Easy, Dr. Benson, let's not let our imaginations run away with us. In a few minutes we will have a better idea of what has happened. Anyway, you know very well there have been times when we have suffered technical difficulties with our satellites, losing their operational capabilities through a variety of glitches. There is a very good chance the satellite will probably be back up and functioning shortly. And as I have said, we should have some new images coming online from our other satellite surveillance and intelligence systems within a few seconds. I have a distinct aversion about jumping to conclusions. Speculation is inherently a colossal waste of time. You know, Dr. Benson, sometimes this can be a slow and tedious process," Colonel Hatch replied in cold formality.

Staff Sergeant Lessard's voice interrupted crisply.

"We have new images coming in from MISTY 2 and 3, Colonel."

Once again, a sudden profound silence descended upon the complex.

"Enhance to full magnification, please," responded Colonel Hatch in a matter-of-fact tone of voice. If she had lost any of her composure, she had regained it rapidly enough. Her demeanor radiated confidence, which had the desired calming effect on everyone around her.

As the deep space images began to appear on the screen, I could feel my heart beating with what seemed like excessive rapidity. For a fleeting moment, I feared others could hear my heartbeat. As I calmed myself, I realized a closer inspection of the screen image could very well confirm my original observations. I had desperately hoped my suspicions were wrong. My observation that the object was surely not among the commonest objects of the universe would be confirmed shortly. I believed this object was from a specific origin, and it entered into our solar system with a specific purpose. I felt sure this was the object of abject horror I had witnessed long ago as a boy. As the images crystallized to a singular clarity, my worst fear was instantly and certainly realized. With the image clearly displayed before us, there was now no doubt the object was a . . . saucer-type spacecraft!

The size of the spacecraft seemed to be a little bit bigger than a professional baseball park's infield, and about two stories tall. It seemed to be made of a brilliant silver alloy of an unknown type. I immediately recognized this spaceship as the one I had observed long ago. The live, streaming images also identified the object as being quite seamless, with no imperfections around the hull of the ship. Beautiful and terrifying to behold, the general majesty of its appearance produced within me a dreadful sentiment of both deep awe and apprehensive anticipation. I was about to speak when the same intense white-light brilliancy suddenly emerged from the spacecraft. As it rushed toward the screen at the same frightful velocity as previously noted, there appeared to be a slight divergence building within the brilliant light. The ray of light was splitting in two! The closer it drew on the screen, the more divergent the paths of light became! That's when the thought abruptly struck me. It has two targets! MISTY 2 and 3!

"Colonel!" I shouted aloud, barely able to contain my excitement. "We must alter the position of MISTY 2 and 3!"

"What the hell are you talking about—"

The excited and high-pitched tone of voice of Staff Sergeant Lessard cut off the colonel's reply.

"Colonel, we have lost visual from MISTY 2!"

"Confirm satellite malfunction, Sergeant," Hatch replied. There was a growing uneasiness and anxiety in her voice, although she tried, without much success, to disguise it. "Switch to secondary satellite imaging. Damn it, I want to know what the hell is going on up there!"

"Colonel Hatch"—I could not be silent any longer—"I have seen this spacecraft before! I am certain our satellite intel systems are being systematically destroyed, eliminated, as it were, with absolute precision by this spaceship! And if my guess is not missing its mark, the Russians and the Chinese intelligence-gathering satellites have probably suffered much the same fate."

"Colonel Hatch!" Staff Sergeant Larry Lessard anxiously interrupted once more, "We have images from MISTY 3 . . . what the hell! Colonel, MISTY 3 is off-line now as well! The screen went blank . . . just like the other two satellite images! We did not receive any kind of signal from these intel satellites that would even begin to indicate or suggest any type of malfunction. Nothing. It's as if they were never there in the first place. Nothing! I just don't understand it."

"I want this facility put on full alert, immediately!" shouted Colonel Hatch to Captain Meyers and Sergeant Huckabee. Tech Sergeant Huckabee pressed a button on her communications panel, and all hell seemed to break loose. Yellow lights began flashing, and a warning siren began wailing its monotonous message. People within the facility began moving at an accelerated pace to wherever they were heading. "Captain, I need a communication link with the space station, now! I want everything we have at our disposal tracking and identifying this object. And, Sergeant Huckabee, get me the Space and Warning Systems Center on the line."

"Attention on deck!" someone shouted aloud.

I turned my head just in time to see the command director, Brigadier General Tom Blackhorne stride past me on his way to the colonel. The general had a startling command presence as he stood a menacing six feet five inches tall. He sported a tightly cropped mustache that, as per military regulations, did not extend beyond the corner of his mouth. The general appeared to be in his early fifties. He was in excellent shape and possessed a red, rough face and a barrel chest. He had assumed command of the Cheyenne Complex facility less than a month ago.

"As you were," responded the general to all in the facility within hearing distance. "Situation report please, Colonel."

"General, we have an unknown object traveling at close to the speed of light toward the Earth's atmosphere, and with apparent hostile intent. Three of our space surveillance satellites were suddenly enveloped in an intense white light, which emanated from the object. All satellites immediately went off-line. We are currently receiving no data type transmissions whatsoever from any of our intel sats. Previous images clearly indicated a saucer-type spacecraft of unknown make and origin. The developing information appears to have placed the unidentified object as having originated from unknown coordinates somewhere near the center of the universe."

"Have we contacted the Space and Warning Systems and NORAD?" asked the general firmly, with a look of annoyed puzzlement on his face.

"Yes, sir. NORAD is on alert and the Space and Warning Systems Center is on the line now," stated Hatch as she looked over at Janet Huckabee, who gave her an affirmative nod.

"Very well, take the phone and let the Space and Warning Systems people know what has happened and what we've seen." Turning his attention to Lessard, the general continued, "Sergeant Lessard, replay those tapes for me, please. I'd like to get a look at this object."

"Yes, sir," replied Lessard as he began the play back.

The general stared at the screen with a steady, cold look in his eyes. With each sequence of extraordinary events unfolding on the screen in front of him, the general's lips drew back convulsively. He grew increasingly solemn and silent.

"They've come back, General." I whispered to the general as I hesitantly took a step toward him at the conclusion of the playback.

"What?" he asked as he swiveled around to face me. His head tilted back cautiously as he gazed suspiciously at me.

"I said they have returned, and I believe with a malevolent purpose."

"Colonel Hatch, who is this civilian, and why is he here?" snapped the general in response to my utterance. It was well known of the general that he possessed a disdain of anything civilian. Especially a civilian working within his military complex.

"General, this is Dr. Robert Benson. He is an astrophysicist and a quantum physicist, and he has the necessary security level clearance. He is here by orders of the Pentagon," said the colonel as she completed her telephone conversation with the Space and Warning Systems Center. "General, I've got the Space and Systems Warning Center standing by for mission support requirements." The colonel then stood and stared at the general, apparently awaiting further orders. But the general still focused his scornful gaze upon me.

"All right, Dr. Benson. If you have some intelligent observations as to what's happening here, now would be an excellent time to share them with us," said General Blackhorne with a sneer and a snort.

"Well, General, at the risk of sounding like a crackpot lunatic, I will," I replied with an indignant tone of voice, as I returned his attention with a hard, cynical stare of my own. An intolerable weight of anxiety began to lift from my mind and body as I spoke. "I was nine years old back in 1951 and living in Washington, D.C., with my mother, Helen, in a common boarding house of the time. A saucer-type spacecraft landed on one of our little league baseball fields in a complex in the park near our house. Thousands witnessed the event, perhaps not as closely as my mother and I had, but—"

"Hold on, Doctor. I have heard of this outrageous story of yours. And as you well know, this event was expressly denied by the U.S. government. According to our government, this event never took place," interrupted the general, his eyes widening suspiciously. The general dismissed my statement with a gesture of impatience then continued.

"I read some of the reports, and all, without exception, stated this event was a hoax. Government sources indicated some sort of mass hysteria involved, a sort of mass hallucination I believe it was called. People who desperately want to start believing in something will, in their own minds, go to the greatest of lengths to make the unreal real. It's sort of a psychological compulsion. Hell, history is littered with examples of that type of thing. If this is the extent of your theories you have to offer, then I think we can muddle through this episode without your help."

"Excuse me, General, but I was there! Nobody is going to tell me what I saw and experienced. Nobody!" I replied, gritting my teeth as a resolute scowl of defiance crossed my face. The general was beginning to disturb me beyond measure. "I believe this spacecraft to be of the same type and origin as the one that landed in Washington, D.C., in 1951. I was nine years old at the time and still remember those events vividly! You don't realize, General, how close we came to a major disaster at that time. In fact, if it weren't for my mother, the Earth may well have been left as a burned-out cinder! That visit was a warning to us not to bring our nuclear capabilities in a hostile manner into outer space. And now, guess what, General? They have returned. Why do you think they have returned to the Earth, General, why? I am absolutely convinced they have come back with a specific intent in mind. The question is, what have we done to merit this hostile return visit? Did we put a nuclear weapons platform in space, General, in blatant defiance of their edict to us? Did we violate the Outer Space Treaty of 1967? Have we provoked a response on their part by a hostile act on our part? Did we, General?"

"As you were, Doctor," barked the general in his command voice. There was more than just a touch of anger in his tone. "You are way out of line! Now, no one is more sorry for what happened to your mother . . ."

"Do not patronize me, General! This has nothing to do with my mother! My present concern is strictly with what is about to happen to our planet. There is more than a good chance that the destruction of the Earth's collective governments is about to occur! I suppose, however, it wouldn't be out of line due to what we and the other idiotic governments of the world have done. Even the United States' detonation of nuclear weapons in outer space beginning with the Teak and Orange shots in 1958 was a violation of the warning. Hell, General, that was only seven years after the warning! Argus I, II, III in 1958! Starfish Prime, Checkmate, and Kingfish in 1962! Plus, let us not forget whatever the Soviets have exploded in space. My god, what have we done?" I cried out as I cover my forehead with the palm of my left hand. My knees felt as if they would buckle at any moment.

"What have we done? We have learned how to protect ourselves, that is what we have done!" snorted the general. "Providing for the common defense of our nation. And further more—"

"General, Colonel, we have the space station on line and are receiving images directly from their photographic systems!" shouted an excited Larry Lessard. "They have their orbiter boom sensor and photo system activated and tracking the object! Unscrambled images are coming in now. We should be able to get a pretty clear picture of whatever is—"

"Put it up on the central display screen, Sergeant," ordered Colonel Hatch, as she cut the sergeant's reply off. "Screen to full magnification, please."

It seemed everyone working in level 5 of the complex immediately shifted their attention to the deep space images being transmitted to Earth by the ISS on the room's enormous computer display screen. This screen's usual purpose was to display the tracking trajectories of all known objects orbiting the Earth. The sudden and alarming appearance of the spacecraft on the large screen elicited a startling gasp from everyone in the room. This was soon followed by a silence of utter bewilderment.

I felt my knees grow weak as I stared at the image on the screen. A sudden, freezing terror gripped me as I was once again struck by the general majesty of its appearance, as well as the possible fiendish malevolence of evil it represented. Like involuntarily viewing a horrifying event, I could not take my eyes off the image. Then, appearing quite abruptly on the screen, the same overlapping ellipses of intense, brilliant light that had radiated outward from the ship before. The brilliant light partially occupied the large screen once again. With each passing second, the intense light grew ominously closer to the viewing point on our screen. As it grew closer, its image grew larger, occupying greater areas of the screen with each second. All personnel, with their eyes riveted upon the screen, seem to be staggering under the visual impact of the unfolding event.

"Oh my god! No!" I shouted aloud. My heart sank as I fully realized we were watching the final moments of the International Space Station along with its five-person crew. With a blinding flash of intense white light, the instant of their destruction was absolute and complete. In my mind's eye, I could imagine an unmistakable disturbance rippling through the quiet vastness of space. As the big screen images disappeared and were replaced by the snowy picture of a lost transmission, Colonel Hatch slowly turned, half hypnotized and with her eyes gently closed, toward Staff Sergeant Lessard. She spoke with a slight quiver in her voice, "Cease transmission to the large display, Sergeant. Resume normal big board tracking operations."

I found myself watching tensely and with heart-sinking despair as General Blackborne imperturbably strode in a silent and quickened pace to the red phone located on the left-hand corner of Sergeant Huckabee's workstation. This telephone was used for one purpose only, and only two people were authorized to use it. As the general picked up the telephone, I knew what would be spoken next.

"Mr. President? This is General Blackborne, Cheyenne Mountain Facility. We have a code-red . . . deep space threat alert. Yes, sir. Three milsatcom destroyed and the International Space Station as well, sir. Yes, sir, I definitely recommend initiating a defensive condition 1 alert. Mr. President, I also recommend commencement of project Dragon-fire on an immediate basis. Yes, sir, he's here. Yes, sir, I understand, Mr. President. Thank you, sir."

The general replaced the telephone receiver in its dark red cradle. He stood momentarily silent then turned to Colonel Hatch.

"Initiate Def-Con 1, Colonel. Alert the Fourteenth Air Force at Vandenburg and the Twentieth at Warren AFB, Wyoming, to stand by for mission intelligence. They will receive their orders and act upon them on my verbal command authority only. By the president's order, I have been authorized to commence Operation Dragon-Fire."

The colonel turned and shouted a command that I could not hear as the din in the complex was accelerating noticeably.

"Colonel, if you please, I need your key authorization," stated General Blackhorne succinctly.

The general then walked over to a little-used console and computer panel, selected a special color-coded key from his key ring. Colonel Hatch quickly performed the same task. Both inserted their respective keys and simultaneously turned them to the right with a vigorous twist. The console lit up like a Christmas tree. As I quickly glanced about, I could see a kind of controlled and ordered chaos playing out around me. I forced myself to move closer to General Blackborne. I did so in spite of an increased aversion to the man, which had been building within me.

"General, just what is Operation Dragon-Fire?" I asked as I felt my nerves stretching tight.

"Since the proverbial cat is about to be let out of the bag, I suppose I could tell you," he replied laconically. "It is our deep space weapons platform that you inquired about previously. Yes, Dr. Benson, we have a deep space weapons platform. So do the Russians, and so do the Chinese as well. Quite frankly, having weapons in space was considered an imperative necessity."

"General, I don't think this is a good idea," I said, as the general abruptly turned his attention back to the control panel.

"For Christ's sake, Dr. Benson, what the hell do you want us to do? Nothing? This thing has come into our space and attacked our satellites. This spaceship has destroyed the space station and its crew. We cannot and will not let that stand. We have considerable technology at our disposal, Dr. Benson, and we are about to give this alien ship a good taste of what we can do."

"Locking on SBL (space borne laser) and DSBM (deep space ballistic missile) Weapons System, now," called out Colonel Hatch. She had donned a portable radio headset, which provided a secure communication link to several different sources. Her voice was once again approaching normality as her military training took over once again.

"General, I know this spaceship! I know what it is capable of doing! Our weapon systems—" I was interrupted by the general once again. His tone of voice was scathing.

"Our weapons system are mid-2011 AFSPC (Air Force Space Command) technology. These are the most up-to-date and powerful weapons systems available to us. The SBL and nuclear tipped DSBM, which are specially designed to be operated in space, will do the job just fine," sneered the general as he pulled a Cuban cigar out of his uniform's pocket.

"General," Colonel Hatch stated flatly as she assumed a position next to the general, "we have a lock on target. All systems are ready for firing."

"Very well, Colonel, fire all designated weapon systems."

"Fire all weapon systems," echoed Colonel Hatch into her radio headset speaker.

"Track results on big display screen, please," the general stated with a somber tone. His expression never changed as he peered intently at the large display screen tracking the paths of both the missiles and the space borne laser. The laser would be the first to strike the spaceship as it could travel at a much faster speed than the missiles. As the concentrated laser beam approached closer to the target, an extraordinary phenomenon began to occur. The laser beam had begun to curve away from the spaceship! The laser beam eventually missed the ship entirely and drifted off into the blackness of deep space. I could see the general grit his teeth as the realization struck him that his weapon had no visible effect on the alien spacecraft. An enhanced analysis performed later would reveal the laser beam missed the spaceship by some one thousand meters, its path deflected by some type of force field.

"SBL missed target," confirmed the voice of Colonel Hatch. "Missiles to impact target in fifty-five seconds." Like everyone in the command section, I could not move my eyes from the screen. I saw the general stiffen to the situation; his face was lined with worry. A profound silence now permeated the atmosphere within the underground facility, producing a faintly unnatural atmosphere. That Colonel Hatch's voice began the fateful countdown.

"Forty-five seconds to impact."

"Thirty-five seconds to impact. Missiles . . . are altering course! Ground control has lost all guidance capabilities!"

A plan so superbly contrived and executed had begun to go awry. A sense of fear seemed to whiten the face of Colonel Hatch. I could see her hands shaking nervously. I stood grim and dismayed. My legs felt weak, as if the Earth was faltering beneath me.

"Detonation in ten," Hatch's voice called out, continuing with her countdown, "nine, eight, seven, six, five, four, three, two, one . . ."

A spectacular explosion seemed to envelope the entire face of the screen. I must admit the nuclear explosion was a thing of beauty and majesty to behold. The intense and brilliant illumination was a boiling mass of a multitude of colors: blue, red, orange, yellow . . . I can't state them all. All colors mixing and broiling together in an awe-inspiring display. I scarcely noticed the misguided eruption of cheering and howling emanating from all points in the large control room. As I looked about, people were slapping each other on the back and congratulating one another. The general, staring intensely at the image on the screen, lit up his tightly wrapped cigar and turned toward me. "I don't think there is much in heaven and Earth that we know of that could survive that explosion, Doctor. Direct hit or not, our nuclear tipped missile was close enough. That was magnificent!"

"I wish I could be as sure as you are, General. But this ship does not come from heaven or Earth. I have a bad feeling that—"

"Look!" Colonel Hatch cried out excitedly as she pointed to the display screen. Out of the broiling mass of color and light emerged the alien spacecraft without a scratch on it. It was as if no explosion had ever taken place against it. In truth, it had not. The same force field, which prevented the laser from striking its target, also deterred the nuclear missile from striking its target. Closer observations would reveal the missile was exploded roughly one hundred miles from its target. The saucer-shaped spaceship continued unscathed on its menacing course toward the Earth. The momentary sense of exaltation flooding the complex was soon replaced by a sense of nightmarish unreality. The general stood silent with his mouth agape for a few seconds then seemed to recover his wits about him.

"Colonel, send all available data to the fourteenth and the twentieth, and let's get everything in the air that we can. Specific intercept and destroy orders," lamented General Blackborne, his voice sounding far away. He turned abruptly toward me, nodded grudgingly, and spoke.

"Dr. Benson, it seems you have more experience with this object than the rest of us. Your knowledge is going to be needed by the president of the United States and the Joint Chiefs of Staff. He has personally ordered you to Washington, D.C. I want you off my facility and on my personal F-22 Raptor within the hour. My Raptor is a specially designed passenger Raptor and is waiting at Peterson AFB outside our gates as we speak. You will be in Washington, D.C., in less than three hours. Please give the president my best regards. Godspeed and good luck."

"And God help us," I said.

A silence fell upon all.

Chapter Two

To Battle

0430
21 Dec 2012
Peterson Air Force Base, Colorado

As we passed through the main gate of Peterson AFB, Colorado, the driver of the jeep I was riding in, who couldn't have been more than nineteen years old, turned unexpectedly toward me and began informing me about the base.

"Doctor, welcome to Peterson Airforce Base, home of the 76th Space Control Squadron," said Sergeant Tom Temple with a widening smile. The sergeant was possessed of chestnut brown hair, a clean-cut face, and glinting eyes. He wore thick, black-framed military glasses, which seem to cover the upper portion of his face, and had an enthusiasm that only the young could display. His lean athletic build was something I had come to expect of everyone in the air force stationed in and around the Cheyenne Mountain Complex. "Peterson Air Force Base is responsible for delivering both defensive and offensive counter-space and space situational awareness in support of any global campaign. The history of this base dates all the way back to World War II. General Claire Chennault formed up the famous "Flying Tigers" on this base. Since that time, we have been a part of a lot of different operations. Hell, we have housed everything from the P-47 Thunderbolt, F-89 Sabre Jet, F-102 Starfighter, to the A-7 and A-10 aircraft. Now, we even have a couple of the most advanced F-22 Raptors based here. Just for your info, Doc, we will be heading to the base operations center to get you oriented and fitted into a flight suit. Once that is accomplished, we'll then get you out to the flight line to board your aircraft. All the prep work is done. For you, everything will be automatic. Piece of cake."

I smiled at his last sentence. So far, nothing about this day has been a piece of cake. Sergeant Peterson began to explain the procedures I would be going through the next hour or so. It seems I would have to skip being briefed on many different aspects of the aircraft, the flight, safety issues, flight suit and helmet fitting, and other areas of expertise, due to the time constraints I found myself under. It seems this was not going to take much time to make this happen, so I resigned myself to being in a constant hurry for the next half hour or so. Due to the extraordinary circumstances we were all functioning under, a rapid departure was the harsh reality. As we approached a building with a Flight Operations sign built into a metal 'A' frame in front of it, I knew the sequence of flight preparation was about to begin.

"Here we are, Doc," smiled Sergeant Peterson as he stopped the jeep. He looked around carefully. The smile suddenly disappeared. "Dr. Benson, what the hell is happening?"

I climbed out of the jeep and stood for a moment looking up at the early morning sky. It seemed the stars were shining extra bright.

"All I can tell you, son, is . . . if I were you, I'd get the hell off this base as rapidly as I could."

While standing beside the F-22 Raptor in my slightly uncomfortable flight suit, I watched with interest as the pilot was performing his visual ground check of the aircraft. I couldn't help but stare in awe at this magnificent machine. The F-22 Raptor, I had been informed while being fitted and slipped into my flight suit, is the most dominant aircraft of its kind. It has been known to fly at supercruise speeds of over 1.5 mach and demonstrate superior maneuverability to any hostile aircraft. Pratt and Whitney's new state-of-the art 35,000 pound-thrust 119 engine supplies enough power for supersonic operation without ever having to use its afterburner. These engines currently outproduce any other known jet engines . . . in any known military. Although it has been speculated the Russians have something similar, there has been no real proof to support that speculation to date. Internal weapon systems allow the Raptor to fly farther, faster, and higher than other fighter aircraft. By its very design, the Raptor significantly reduces the aerodynamic drag effect known to slow down any aircraft. The F-22 also possesses a highly stealthy signature that makes it almost impossible for enemy tracking systems to find and follow. Also, the jet's sensor system allows it to find, target, and kill an enemy aircraft before the enemy aircraft even has a chance to detect the Raptor. With a 1,724-mile range, I figured we would need a bit of refueling from a KC-135 to safely reach Washington, D.C., for my conference with the president. My thoughts surrounding this marvelous aircraft were eventually interrupted by my pilot for the journey.

"Dr. Benson? I am Major Jack Holloway. I will be escorting you to our nation's capital today," said a fairly tall, athletic-looking man as he extended his hand toward me. While shaking his hand, I couldn't help but notice he was possessed of a strong, self-assured grip. Jack Holloway epitomized fighter pilots of the day. He was confident, perhaps a little arrogant, and had a keen eye for details. His jet-black hair was neatly trimmed in the true military regulation manner. I instantly realized I was in very good hands for this morning's trip to our America's capital.

"Nice to meet you, Major," I responded sincerely, as I let go of the major's hand.

"I understand you're an important piece of cargo, Doctor," he replied without changing his expression as the ground crew moved the ladder for boarding the aircraft into position at the cockpit. He continued in a voice that was uncompromising and clear, "It is my job to get you to your destination safely and as rapidly as possible. Now, if you'll please follow the instructions of the ground crewman, we'll get you strapped into the aircraft and squared away for the trip. We should be departing around 0810 hours and arriving, with the time zone changes, about 1200 hours.

I followed the major's command, and within a few moments, I was sitting in the passenger seat situated directly behind pilot's seat of the specially designed Raptor. It was a tight fit, fairly claustrophobic, but the excitement of the impending Raptor ride was countermanding any fleeting feeling of discomfort. The ground crewman adjusted my harness. It was so tight; it felt as if I couldn't move a muscle even if I had wanted. The crewman demonstrated how to use the ejector-seat switch in case of emergency then tapped me on the shoulders and gave me the thumbs up sign. Soon the major was strapped in as well, and I nearly had an accident in my flight suit as the roar of the two Pratt and Whitney engines came abruptly to life. Eventually, the Raptor began to taxi toward the runway for takeoff. As it was truly starting to become bright out, I flipped my sunshield visor down. The oxygen mask was tight against my face, and my breathing was a bit choppy and labored in anticipation of the takeoff. The nose of the F-22 Raptor was soon pointed down the beginning of the long runway. We held there for a brief moment.

"All right, Doc, hold on to your gonads," came the voice of Major Holloway through the radio-intercom. "Here we go!"

I heard the engines thunder as the aircraft jolted abruptly and the runway began passing rapidly under our aircraft. As the Raptor's nose pulled upward, we roughly rose and darted into the air. I felt myself pushed heavily against the back of my seat, as the force of gravity began weighing heavily upon me. I watched the altimeter with some amazement as we rapidly climbed to a cruising altitude of approximately 45,000 feet. If I was reading the airspeed gauge correctly, our speed was approximately 1.5 mach.

"God, this is awesome," I muttered as I gazed at the beauty all around me. The sun was in full magnificence, with a wisp of clouds passing directly below our aircraft. The Colorado mountains were rapidly disappearing from view, being slowly replaced by a more level ground.

"I never get tired of it," Major Holloway said amiably. "Man, I love my job!"

I guess I had forgotten that the major could hear me through the mask's radio microphone, for I had not expected a reply or a comment. I was finally becoming more comfortable and acclimated to my surroundings, and the noise of the aircraft's engines seemed to have settled into a loud but rhythmic drone. The hypnotic drone of the Raptor's engines were effectively working to put me to sleep. I just remembered that I haven't slept for probably thirty hours or so, and I soon found myself nodding off, reawakening, then nodding off again. It was during one of the nodding off times when the voice of Major Holloway startled me awake. There was an urgency in the tone of his voice that immediately got my attention.

"Doctor, I'm switching you over to my radio frequency. You have a message coming in from Cheyenne Mountain."

"Dr. Benson," the voice, strained and nervous, was that of Colonel Hatch, "we initiated another strike on the object through Dragon-Fire, with the same results. No damage done. It was shortly after our strike attempt that we lost communication with the deep space weapons platform. All indications are that it was completely destroyed by the object. This spaceship has completely shredded our defenses. We have nothing left to stop it from entering into our atmosphere, and that event should be occurring very shortly. We are in the process of scrambling all available fighter jets to intercept, over."

"Understood, Colonel. Have we got a fix on the spaceship's current trajectory, over," I replied, as I could feel my face wrinkle in thought under the weight of my oxygen mask. I was desperately searching my memory for some forgotten fact that could be of some small benefit to the colonel. Unfortunately, it only took a moment to realize I had virtually no information that could be of use.

"Coming in now, Doctor. It seems we may be catching a break on this one," Colonel Hatch continued with a loud, high-pitched voice. "Seems its current course should bring it down somewhere over the sea of Japan, Korea, or China. Hard to pinpoint an exact location at this time. As we get more updated information, I should be able to give you a more accurate answer, over."

"All right, colonel. I suggest you speak with the general about an immediate evacuation of the Cheyenne Mountain Complex," I said in an urgent and decisive tone, wanting to emphasize and underscore my next statement to her. "Unless there is a significant flaw in my reasoning, the spaceship destroying our satellites and weapons platform probably has the capabilities to accurately trace back to the source just who is directing those attacking systems. In my opinion, everyone in the complex is in extreme danger. You need to get your people out of there. I would also suggest an immediate evacuation of Peterson Air Force Base, over."

"Roger that," she replied, "I'll bring it up to the CO immediately. However, my bet is he will resist the idea. Good luck on your meeting with the president. Hatch out."

"Dr. Benson, what in the hell is going on?" asked Major Holloway anxiously, as soon as my transmission with Cheyenne Complex had concluded.

"Major, without trying to sound too overly melodramatic, I'm afraid it could very possibly be the end of our world as we know it. Our deep space sensors and imaging systems suddenly picked up an alien spacecraft traveling at tremendous speeds. Shortly thereafter, the object swiftly neutralized our maelstroms and also destroyed the space station. Apparently the object did not appreciate our efforts to observe it, nor was it particularly pleased with our attempts to destroy it. This unknown object was later observed to be a saucer-type spaceship. We tried to halt its progress through the use of our deep space weapons platform, but unfortunately those efforts fell short as well. The spaceship now seems to be proceeding toward a landing somewhere around the region of Asia. Major, if my calculations are correct, this event seems to be fulfilling a prophecy from 1951. An incident in which I was directly involved. Due to the advanced technology possessed by the alien, all of our weapons will be rendered useless against this threat. I wish I was mistaken, but I don't think there is going to be a snowball's chance in hell of stopping this spaceship. However, I don't think my opinion is shared by those in power. Unfortunately, that fact is going to get a lot of good people killed uselessly."

"A prophecy from 1951? What in the hell are you talking about?" he asked with more curiosity in his voice than bewilderment.

"This particular spacecraft first visited us back in 1951. Hundreds . . . thousands of people saw it. Since that time, our government has not only disavowed the event but has worked tirelessly in an effort to prove every one who saw this ship was an idiot, on drugs, hallucinating, or just an enemy of the government. Thousands were threatened, some were displaced, some were harassed, and some even hounded out of their homes and cities. Those who refused to comply with the government's wishes were arrested by those same government agents. Some people just turned up missing and were never heard from again. Our government, along with other governments of the world conspired to eliminate all knowledge of this event. All governments of the world are guilty, and quite frankly, there are no limitations or bounds on what each government will do to maintain itself in power. Rest assured, Major, when a government passes unpopular laws on an unwilling public in an effort to stay in power, and cares not about the people who elected it into power, then that government must necessarily destroy itself in the process. In this case, the governments of Earth have run out of time to self-destruct. Now, because of their evil actions, they have brought destruction on themselves in the form of an extraterrestrial source. The most unfortunate aspect of this scenario is the governments of the world will quite possibly destroy millions of their own people in the process. Due to these government's criminal, thoughtless, and selfish actions, I am convinced the civilizations of our world are about to face complete and utter annihilation. You see, Jack, we were specifically warned back in 1951 not to extend our violent behavior into outer space. The Earth's governments did not heed the warning."

I took a moment to breathe deeply then continued.

"In my opinion, once our government became overrun with lawyers turned politicians, bad things started to happen. It would have been much preferred, in my opinion, if the first law we passed as a newly formed nation was, no one who had any background in law would ever be permitted to serve in any capacity, in any governmental department. These lawyers have been the ruin of us all. It is my considered opinion that the United States hasn't won a war or a conflict since lawyers started writing the rules of engagement. We became more afraid of getting sued than winning a war! Our military members began to be more afraid of being hauled up in front of a congressional hearing or a court martial on some trumped up charge, initiated by the enemy, no less, than they were of fighting in combat. They feared being roasted as some sort of sacrificial lamb by some congressman or senator trying to look noble. Military members began to fear our own senators and congressmen more than they feared waging an aggressive war against a deranged, dangerous, and determined enemy."

"Well, I can't disagree with you there, Doc," replied the Major acidly, as a sense of anger and disgust rose in his voice. "Doc, I got to agree with you. The United States started losing wars and battles when we permitted lawyers, instead of military personnel, to write the rules of engagement. Hell, in my opinion there shouldn't be any rules of engagement. The very last thing anyone should want to do is . . . to go to war. Diplomacy, discussion, begging, whatever, should always be tried first. If, and when, those efforts fail, and the safety of our people and our country are truly threatened, then and only then do we go to war. And once we go to war, damn it, then let us fight it as a war. Destroy the enemy's troops, its factories, its cities, its towns, and its people. None of this precision strike bullshit! That has never worked, and it never will. It is silly and criminal for our politicians to send our young men and women into harm's way then tie their hands behind their back and tell them you cannot shoot unless fired upon. You cannot return fire and destroy the enemy in their mosques, hospitals, homes . . . or whatever. As General Sherman put it, "War is hell!" and, it should be waged as such until every last one of your enemy is destroyed . . . men, women, and children. If we fought war that way, maybe there would be less wars."

"Well said, Major Holloway. However, I'm afraid that what is about to happen to this planet, and its people will make all of our theoretical arguments a moot point," I replied, speaking slowly as I thought. "Major, have you ever read the Bible?"

"Back where I grew up in the South, it was damn near required reading, Doc. Why?" he replied, his curiosity aroused.

"I was just thinking about the fact that God has almost always given his children a warning before punishing them. For instance, he told Lot to get the good people out of Sodom and Gomorrah before he destroyed the cities, along with all their inherent evil. The same with Noah and the ark. It seems to me that God has warned mankind over and over again about man's evil ways, and we have always stubbornly refused to listen. Perhaps now it is too late. Perhaps now his avenging angel has come once again. Maybe for the final time," I said dejectedly, and with great sorrow, as a sense of despair descended upon me.

"Hey, lighten up, Doc," came the booming voice of Major Holloway. "You're beginning to creep me out. This alien intruder was not sent from God. We can stop him. We can defeat him. Never bet against the underdog, Doc. Remember the story of David and Goliath."

"Yes, I remember. But David had God on his side. Unfortunately, I believe we may not enjoy the same blessing as David. In fact, the current liberal and progressive politicians in our country, and the ACLU, among others, have gone a long ways toward kicking God out of our country in a misguided effort for the majority to please the minority. Hell, one man who is an atheist states he doesn't want his kid subjected to prayer in school, and right away our courts nullify the rights of the other twenty-nine kids in the class who want to pray to their God. It's ridiculous! The United States of America was founded on Judeo-Christian principles and beliefs, not any other. Show me where the name of Mohammed or Hussein was signed anywhere on our constitution. Our elected politicians have sold us out. They sold our country down the drain in order to put a little coin into their pockets. Name me one politician today who isn't a millionaire? Do you realize if a man or a woman gets elected to congress and serves their four- or six-year term, they are now eligible for a large pension the rest of their lives? Hell, military members must survive at least twenty years' service to even qualify for a small pension."

With my last comment, both the major and I seemed to become lost in our own quiet observations and thoughts. I am quite sure Major Holloway could tell I was pretty bitter about what had become of our once-great country. My rancorous thoughts, however, began to dissolve once again due to the lulling effect of the constant drone from the two Pratt and Whitney engines. The sound began to slowly hypnotize me, wearing me down as I drifted ever closer to blessed sleep once again. Soon, my thoughts eventually trailed off into a deep sleep as fatigue overwhelm all my senses. I don't know how long I slept, but I was suddenly jolted awake by the strong voice of Major Holloway.

"Time to wake up, Doc," he said with a chuckle. "Hell, I wouldn't have known you had drifted off to sleep if I hadn't heard you snoring on the intercom! Anyway, we'll be landing in a few minutes. There is a helicopter standing by to fly you to the White House. Hope you enjoyed flying Raptor Airways, and we do hope you'll travel with us again."

"The honor and pleasure was all mine, Major," I responded, expressing my sincere gratitude for the major's exemplary flying skills and the excellent conversation. I soon felt a small jolt as the landing gear hydraulically lowered and locked itself into position. The runway was rising rapidly up to meet us, and soon, with a bump and a short squeal of rubber meeting the road, we were safely on the ground and taxiing to our predetermined parking area. The roar of the engines swiftly died down as we came to a complete halt. As I undid my face mask, the bubble-type canopy slid quietly open. Two airman moved to secure a ladder into place on the side of the Raptor for Major Holloway and me to disembark from the aircraft. It briefly occurred to me I must have slept through the mid-air refueling of our aircraft. Once safely upon the ground, I did a few squats to get my land legs back, turned, and bid a fond farewell to Major Holloway.

"Jack," I stated with a smile, squinting against the late morning sun, "Thanks for the ride and the conversation. I enjoyed them both."

"Anytime, Doc. Be seeing you."

I was then escorted away by one of the two young airman. As we started to proceed toward a dark blue helicopter setting in its circled landing pad, I glanced up and noticed the helicopter's rotor blades beginning their initial rotation. The whirring sound was accompanied by an awakened roar of the helicopter's engine. Revolving slowly at first, the rotor blades rapidly gained in speed. The airman accompanying me turned toward me and spoke in a rather loud voice, cupping his mouth with his hands so I could hear him over the increasing whine of the helicopter's engine.

"Dr. Benson, I have orders to board you immediately. You will be at the White House in about twenty minutes. Good luck with your mission, sir."

"Thanks," I replied as I clambered aboard the helicopter. The aircraft's crew chief moved swiftly to belt me in then turned and gave a thumbs up signal to the pilot compartment. Almost immediately, we were under way as we lifted off effortlessly into the smoggy afternoon air. Not a word was spoken to me throughout the flight. However, I did enjoy listening to the pilots speak to ground control and to the crew of the helicopter. I wistfully recalled I hadn't been aboard a helicopter since my Marine Corps days at Camp Pendleton in the early 1960s.

Upon landing, I was met by the White House chief of staff Scott Bryant. Scotty, as he was affectionately known, was a tall, somber man with a thin face. He wore wire-rimmed glasses and sported a well-cropped moustache. His chestnut brown hair was neatly cropped as well, and he was dressed impeccably in a blue suit and tie to match. After thanking the pilots and crew of the helicopter, we walked quickly toward the famed White house. Mr. Bryant began informing me on the schedule of events.

"Dr. Benson, you will meet with the president and his chiefs of staff, including the chairman of the Joint Chiefs of Staff of the military, in approximately one hour. You look pretty well done in, so I will take you to the VIP shower facilities to get cleaned up and refreshed, then to the cafeteria for a quick bite to eat."

"Sounds good, Scott. I could use a nice hot shower and some food. I swear I cannot remember when I had last eaten anything."

The VIP restroom and shower facilities were quite luxurious. They were spacious and had beautiful light brown marble tile, which contained darker brown swirls through them. The shower area itself was large and comfortable, with several different bathing areas, and all of them came equipped with body-wash jets. The warm water and body spray absolutely rejuvenated my body and spirits, and soon I was feeling refreshed and invigorated.

As I dried off, I noticed that a new suit had been laid out and prepared for me, and as I began dressing, I thought "someone did their job very well," as the clothes fit perfectly. I had just finished buttoning up the suit jacket when Scott Bryant walked into the outer alcove. I knew from all the news accounts that Scott had a reputation for unfailing precision in his duties, and as such he returned to escort me to the small cafeteria within the VIP quarters of the White House.

"May I suggest the ravioli?" he stated in a modest and unassuming manner as we entered the small cafeteria. "The chef today is part Italian, and his ravioli and meat sauce are as good as you can get anywhere in the world. Add a salad and a small loaf of his homemade Italian bread, and you have a very tasty meal. One that is fit for a king."

"I think that altogether agrees with me, Scott. The ravioli it is, then," I said as I could feel my appetite begin to rise at the mere aroma of the ravioli and meat sauce. I grabbed an iced tea with lemon and proceeded to a nearby table. Scott sat down opposite me with his plate of ravioli and opened up a discussion soon after downing his first few bites of the delicious ravioli.

"We will be meeting with the president in the situation room. This is a medium-sized conference room in the west wing of the White House. You will see that this room has a large amount of video screens within it for the display of all types of information and data. These screens can be used for secure video teleconferencing or used to display real-time data for analysis by the president and senior personnel. The situation room is exclusively reserved for National Security Council meetings and other senior level White House meetings and briefings, along with any national emergency that may arise from time to time. And this shocking occurrence certainly qualifies as one of those times. We also use this room frequently for videoconferencing with the president when he is traveling to all points of the globe. It can be used on a daily basis to provide both secure and nonsecure information and data to senior decision makers within the government in an effort to assist them in their decision making process. I think you will find the situation room to be a state-of-the-art, twenty-first century facility capable of monitoring events around the world, and also in space. Joining the briefing in the situation room today, will be the vice president, the chairman of the Joint Chiefs of Staff, the directors of the FBI, the CIA, Homeland Security, and the National Security Council. The secretary of state and the secretary of Defense will also be in attendance."

"Sounds like a full house," I said as I stuffed another fork full of ravioli in my mouth. The ravioli was tender, and the sauce was sweet. "Tell me Scott, what is my role in all this?"

"The president has been informed you may have some personal information about what we are up against and desires your counsel on the matter. We need to do some problem solving, and I don't think we have much luxury of time to accomplish it."

"What is the current status of the spaceship? Where's it at? What's been happening?" I asked Scott as I sipped on my iced tea. I could notice my strength returning with each bite of food I consumed.

Scott finished sipping his iced tea and slowly set it down on the table. He let out a low sigh, eyes glinting to the right then left. He hesitated then leaned forward.

"The spacecraft has landed in Pyongyang, North Korea," he whispered. His eyes narrowed as his voice grew quieter. "So far, there is no further activity from the landing site . . . yet. There is also something else I have been approved by the highest confidential sources to tell you, Dr. Benson. Shortly after entering the Earth's atmosphere and tracking over our continent, we abruptly lost communication with the Cheyenne Mountain Complex. No NORAD, no U.S. Space Command, no Space and Warning Systems, nothing. The president immediately ordered a search and rescue team to the site, but by the time they arrived . . ."

"They reported the complex had been totally destroyed." I finished the sentence for him as I felt a sinking feeling in the pit of my stomach. He lifted an eyebrow and nodded.

"Yes. And not only that, we have since lost all communication with our fleet of nuclear-powered submarines operating in the Pacific Ocean! We attempted a search and rescue mission with some very high-tech ships designed for such a purpose, but they all stalled about twenty-five miles out to sea. Engines just suddenly stopped and refused to restart . . . on each and every ship! It was the damnest thing. There was no apparent reason for those engines to fail," replied Scott, banging his index finger upon the tabletop to emphasize his point.

It took only a moment for me to realize the full import of his statements. There was a distinct pause in the conversation as I slowly pushed my empty plate to the middle of the table.

"Losses?" I asked as I lowered my head into the palm of my hands.

"The word *catastrophic* comes immediately to mind," responded Scott in a flat tone. His facial expression did not change. "But they could have been worse. Thanks to your timely suggestion to Colonel Hatch, they were able to evacuate some of the more nonessential personnel, admin clerks, cooks, cleaning crew, before some sort of high-intensity energy beam hit the complex. From what I've been told, the remaining crew inside the complex were vaporized. Nothing left of them except some ashes. And I mean only a small amount of ashes. This energy beam weapon—"

"Scotty," I interrupted as I leaned forward and pushed myself up and away from the table. My knees suddenly felt like they were turning to water, "I think it's time for me to see the president."

Scott followed my lead and stood up. He swiftly grabbed our trays and moved away from the dining table. After Scott dropped off our trays, I followed him out into the long, expansive hallway, which eventually led into a medium-sized anti-room. After Scott closed the door, he waved me to a row of chairs next to the far wall.

"If you will please wait here, Dr. Benson, I will announce your arrival to the president and his staff," Scott said as he opened the door only slightly. He deftly slid through the small opening, disappearing into the situation room, the large door closing securely behind him.

I slowly let my body sink into the chair closest to door in which Scott had disappeared. I suddenly felt very, very old.

Chapter Three

Gort

1310
21 Dec 2012
Washington, D.C.

The door to the situation room suddenly opened, and Scott Bryant stuck his head and shoulders out through the opening.

"The president is ready to see you now, Dr. Benson," he said formally, in a low, steady voice. I quickly rose from my chair and followed Scott into the White House situation room. As I entered the room, I could see the president acknowledge my entrance, rise from his chair, and begin to walk toward me. I must confess, he looked a bit smaller than I had imagined, but his well-known features and somewhat somber face were quite prominent. He was the very portrait of a troubled man in apparent deep thought. He seemed very much a gaunt and unhappy-looking person with the weight of his country on his shoulders. The small tuffs of grey hair on his head were striking signs of the stress and pressure of the office. I do not remember him looking this way when he was elected. The office does seem to age each man who occupies it.

"Mr. President, this is Dr. Robert Benson," began Scott in a formal manner. "Dr. Benson, the president of the United States."

"Dr. Benson, I am happy you could join us this evening. I look forward to your input on the crisis facing our great nation, and the world," said the president as he permitted himself a small, quick smile toward me. He put his hand on my shoulder and began to guide me toward the others in the situation room. "Let me introduce you to our gathering here today."

The president of the United States in quick succession formally introduced me to the vice president of the United States, the chairman of the Joint Chiefs of

Staff, the director of the CIA, the director of the FBI, the director of Homeland Security, the department chief of the National Security Council, the secretary of state, and the secretary of Defense. After I solemnly shook hands with each of them, the president motioned me to have a seat across from where he was sitting at a large conference table.

As I began my initial scan of the situation room, I noticed there were multiple computers and screens or monitors located throughout the room. Some, apparently had the same function, others with an altogether different function to perform. I was momentarily stunned by the number and quality of the sophisticated computers and communications equipment dispersed throughout the area. I swiftly realized this was an illogical reaction considering the environment in which I now found myself. The president motioned to me with an automatic gesture toward the chair obviously reserved for me. As we sat down, I stared intently at the president, waiting for his opening remarks. I didn't have long to wait.

"Dr. Benson, I thought it important to have you here since you seem to have some preeminent knowledge about this spaceship, its possible mission here, and, more importantly, its capabilities. Therefore, I will immediately yield the floor to you. Please speak freely," the president said in a flat and somber tone as he leaned back in his plush, executive, leather chair. I felt the piercing, hard, cynical eyes of everyone within the situation room settling suspiciously upon me. I could not help but sense an underlying tone of hostility toward me. I was very much a stranger in a strange land.

"Mr. President," I said, with a difficult effort to remain calm, cool, and collected as I responded to the president's statement, "It is my considered opinion that this country, no . . . the entire world, is in grave peril. The unexpected and alarming appearance of this spacecraft is not without a meaning. It is most certainly not without an objective. From the very moment the object entered into our long range, deep space surveillance and intelligence systems, its movement and its actions have communicated quite clearly its intentions toward our planet. In short, Mr. President, I believe its mission is to destroy every nuclear-related facility on the Earth. To what degree it intends to wreak destruction upon us . . . is unknown. Will it destroy every living thing on the Earth? Will it visit upon us some sort of lesser destruction? I can only theorize, based upon my careful calculations and observations as to why the spaceship has returned. But if my theories are correct, then every country which possesses nuclear power, nuclear energy, or is developing those capabilities will most certainly be targeted."

With eyebrows raised, the president exchanged glances with everyone in the room but remained silent. He returned the intensity of his gaze back to me but still remained silent. As I quickly glanced about the room and was not questioned by anyone, I assumed this to be a signal for me to continue. I locked my eyes once again on the president.

"If the president remembers correctly, the people of Earth were visited by a similar spacecraft in 1951. At that time, the alien emissary aboard the ship issued a warning to all the people of Earth. The governments of the world have since failed to heed the warning, or even take it seriously. I do not know how or why that happened, but it did. And now, either the very same spacecraft, or one very similar in nature, has again landed on our world. This time, there is a definite and unmistakable, hostile intent. I believe the spacecraft has returned to exact a severe punishment on the people of Earth for failing to heed—"

"Excuse me, Dr. Benson," interrupted the voice of the secretary of Defense. "According to all history that I have ever read, Earth has never been visited by any type of alien life-form. The official government reports and policies—"

"The event I allude to did, in actuality, happen in 1951 as I have previously stated. This occurred at what was then known as the President's Park, right here in Washington, D.C.," I interjected indignantly against the implied accusation, tapping my index finger on the table to emphasize my point.

"Dr. Benson"—now the voice was that of Vice President—"if you are seriously suggesting and referring to . . ."

"I am," I responded with a rising note of anger in my voice. What initially had been people with alert and receptive minds had now seemed to have descended quickly into outright scorn and contempt. I continued with dogged determination.

"Believe me, I am all too aware that our government, one administration after the other, has disavowed any knowledge the incident took place. My mother was harassed and hounded to her death by one lying administration after another, pursuing their policies of obfuscation and deceit. Well, I must admit all of you in our government have done your job very well. The politicians running our government's first concern was themselves, and not, first and foremost, the American people they are supposed to serve. As with most government people, their primary avocation is to do whatever is necessary to stay in power. Disregarding the truth of past events merely to stay in power and lord over the American people is reprehensible. Only now, guess what, everyone? It has come back to bite us right in the ass."

"That's it, Mr. President, I think we have heard enough of Dr. Benson's remarks," interrupted the vice president once again, in a loud and sarcastic tone of voice. I fully realized I did not at that moment have a friend in the room. Perhaps, more importantly, I did not care. I was not about to start pulling punches against the very people who contributed to promoting this crisis. To his credit, the president silenced all dissent with a curt wave of his hand.

"Please, everyone," responded the president as he surveyed the faces surrounding him, "I want to hear him out. We need to hear all points of view, and all possible options. I know a lot of this may be hard for us to hear, but hear it we must. If Dr. Benson is correct in his observations, then he may, indeed, be our best source of information about this alien threat. If he is incorrect, then that, too, should be born out shortly. Please, Dr. Benson, continue."

"Thank you, Mr. President. I am acutely aware this is not something anyone wants to hear. Nor am I saying this with any other motive in mind than to impress upon you the precariousness of our situation. We are all in this dangerous situation together, and the decisions coming out of this conference, out of this administration, could very well mean life or death to millions of American people, not to mention billions of other people throughout the world. If I sound like I—"

"Excuse me! But would everyone focus their attention on screen 3!" interrupted the director of the CIA, pointing to a screen displaying real-time images of the alien spacecraft's landing site in North Korea. "I apologize for the interruption, but there is definitely something happening with the spacecraft!"

The rounded dome of the saucer-type space ship began to slowly open. The top of the ship's curvature parted in a vertical manner, at the central apex of the dome. Where there was no previous evidence of a seam or crease in the ship's hull, the triangular opening grew. Simultaneously, a small walkway began to push itself out from the lower portion, or the base, of the dome on the sauce-shaped ship. The dazzling, silver metallic pathway seemed to effortlessly slide out from the main hull of the ship until it became a smooth seamless entranceway into the ship.

As I looked at the screen in fascination, I managed to tear my gaze momentarily from the terrifying images, and managed a quick glance at several of the other screens situated around the room. Most of the screens were now portraying what was happening in North Korea. Some, however, were displaying the event at different photographic angles, so there were slightly different images showing on each screen. I noticed on one of the images, the North Korean Army units surrounding the spaceship had come to full alert, with weapons raised. There were no signs of vehicles or artillery pieces. The Korean Army units had only come on foot. I found myself staring intently at the screen in front of me in awe, wonder, and perplexity. As my sense of foreboding increased, a startling and terrifying form began to slowly emerge from the bowels of the ship. With each slow step of the specter, my knees shook uncontrollably. I gasped aloud in sheer horror when I fully observed the apparition upon the screen. Shaking myself out of the sudden state of heart-sinking despair I found myself in, I managed to utter only one word.

"Gort!"

I could scarcely breathe as I watched the absolutely fascinating but dreadful sequence of events unfold before my eyes. The robot stood a full eight feet tall. Its body was as seamless and metallic as its spaceship. Gort appeared exactly as I remembered. The deadly robot had a large frightening helmet for its head. Where the eyes would have been on a human, there existed upon Gort a large visor that connected to some sort of earpiece on either side of the robot's huge head. The earpiece consisted of three circular rings mounted on top of each other, each one smaller than the one it rested upon. The great square jaw of the headpiece connected securely and seamlessly to its strong neck. Two arms formed themselves out of its great square shoulders, ending in the hands of the robot, which were encased into a sort of metallic mitten, with the thumb separate from the rest of the smooth, seamless appendage.

The robot had thick cuffs around the wrists and also had some type of a midsection belt around its waist. Below the large belt was what best can be described as a triangular loin section of the unknown metal. The robot's large legs extruded from the loin section. The robot's oversized, shiny metal boots upon which it stood were of a seamless perfection as well. Altogether, the robot was at once a horrible, but magnificent sight to behold. Everyone within the situation room was solemn and silent. The only sound I could hear was that of my own heartbeat.

Gort moved slowly and methodically. Step by small measured step, the robot strode down the walkway of the ship to the ground. Gort suddenly halted its forward movement a few paces in front of the pathway and stood momentarily motionless. The North Korean Army stood its ground. Then, with an evil and agonizing slowness, the visor on Gort's helmet began to lift upward, sliding back into the interior of the helmet. The visor continued to slide upward into his helmet until it completely disappeared. A small, but intense and brilliant, white light became visible from within the robot's opened visor. The light began to pulsate in a hypnotically slow, rhythmic pattern. I only had seconds to mentally brace myself against the fiendish malevolence I knew was about to occur. The faint echoes of an impending comment died in my throat. I did not have the ability to speak. Anyway, I wanted the full impact of what I knew was about to happen to be completely absorbed by those around me.

A small but sharp stream of intense, white light abruptly shot forward from the middle of the visor opening. The energy beam broke into many smaller streams of light that impacted the soldiers of the North Korean army surrounding the ship. The white light grew so intense in its brilliancy that it fully enveloped our viewing screens. The brilliance maintained itself on screen for a matter of about thirty seconds. For those few precious moments, we could observe nothing. The profound silence and awe within the situation room was maintained until the brilliancy of the light upon the screen slowly began to dissipate. As the horrific scene began to appear before our eyes, several gasps of terrified awe and utter bewilderment swept through the room. The North Korean Army units and all their weapons had simply vanished. What remained was only shadows of burnt and scorched earth where men and vehicles had once stood. The visor upon Gort's helmet slowly lowered back into its original place. The spectacle was fascinating in its simplicity and sheer horror. The profound silence that had descended upon the room was deafening. Every eye in the room was riveted to the screens. It was a full ten seconds before the silence in the room was shattered.

"Oh, my God," uttered the president in a scarcely perceptible voice.

Once again, as if in response to the president's exclamation, Gort was on the move. The robot took three or four steps, turning his metal body toward the presidential palace area of central Pyongyang. Once again, his visor slowly raised into the open position, and the pulsating, intense light became visible. Small pinpoint streams of the intense, brilliant light suddenly emerged from the robot until it again fully enveloped the viewing screen. The people assembled in the situation room remained silent as the dreadful scene began to play itself out. As soon as the brilliant flare of light dissipated, the overall destruction of the city of Pyongyang shocked even the heartiest and bravest of souls in the room. Where once a thriving city of a million and a half people stood, there now could be seen an area of complete and utter devastation.

Everything had been vaporized in a matter of seconds. An image of desolation comparable to the surface of the moon was now confronting the president and his staff. The same scorched earth could be seen for miles in any direction. No buildings, no bridges, no people, no plant or animal life could be seen to still exist. Everyone stared disbelievingly at the screen, staggering at the visual impact of the catastrophe. After this second display of awesome might and power, no one dared speak for what seemed like a matter of minutes. All horrified eyes remained riveted to the screens in the situation room.

"Mr. President"—the silence was eventually broken by the steady voice of the director of the CIA, who had apparently commenced to receive some information across his communications networks—"we are starting to receive some preliminary reports from what is left of our ground sources. Apparently, all of central Pyongyang has been obliterated. We can with some degree of certainty also confirm the destruction of the MGC-20 Cyclotron Research and Development Center and the Pyongyang Underground Nuclear Power Plant as well. All of the North Korean governmental buildings and the presidential palace has been destroyed. Early indications are . . . a total eradication of all government and nuclear facilities within this area."

"May I take a moment to point out the robot has turned and is heading back into the ship," came the calm and expressionless voice of the National Security Council section head. Everyone's eyes once again peered fixed and motionless at the screen. The observation was absolutely correct. The robot had turned and walked back up the smooth, elevated platform leading into the ship until the robot was soon lost from sight. The spaceship had returned back to its original state. No pathway, opening, or seam at all could be discerned. It was only a few moments after the observation was made that the spacecraft began to glow with a strange but beautiful pulsating light, which radiated out from underneath the spaceship. Then, quite unexpectedly, the ship lifted off the ground and commenced to move in a north by northeast direction.

"Are we able to track it?" asked the president to no one in particular. The secretary of Defense answered the president after a brief pause.

"Although the object destroyed all of our military satellite systems when it first entered our solar system and the Earth's atmosphere, it did not destroy some of the world's communication satellites. Plus, we can tap into some North Korean ground-feed capabilities as well. We should be able to track and observe it for the time being. However, I should mention we have no guarantee as to how long we can maintain surveillance."

"Mr. President," interrupted the CIA director, "the spacecraft is slowing for an apparent landing in the area of the Yongbyon Nuclear Complex. I can't believe how rapidly it covered the sixty miles from Pyongyang to Yongbyon! It was just a few seconds . . ." His voice trailed off.

The spaceship landed within the middle of the Yongbyon Nuclear complex. Once the spaceship had landed and became stationary, it was only a few seconds before the dome of the craft opened and Gort menacingly reappeared. Some of the North Korean soldiers guarding the complex had rapidly assembled around the spacecraft. They were the first to be vaporized by the robot. They had given their lives honorably, willingly and . . . uselessly, unable to escape the death that cut them down. Within only a matter of a few minutes, the declared waste storage facility, 50MW Nuclear Power Plant, the undeclared waste storage facility and the radiochemistry laboratory ceased to exist in the blinding white light.

The south end of the compound containing the Fuel Fabrication Complex also was abruptly obliterated by the earth-scorching beam of intense energy. The final target area for Gort's assault was the immediate vicinity of the northern sector, containing the 5MW(e) Experimental Reactor, the Yongbyon Nuclear Research Center, and the IPT2000 Nuclear Research Reactor. At an almost inconceivable speed, Yongbyon had disappeared from the face of the Earth leaving behind a desolated and devastated scene of complete and total destruction. There was no life to be seen anywhere around the area. No birds, no dogs, no insects . . . nothing. Gort had completed his destructive work without concern for any form of life. The devastation was so thorough, the remaining charred fragments were almost meaningless to the eye. Gort, the alien galaxy's grim guardian against aggression, turned and gradually began his way back into the interior of his spacecraft.

"I don't understand," said the CIA director after a few moments, "where the hell is the North Korean Air Force? Where are their ballistic missiles?"

"Perhaps," I started to no one in particular, searching for a satisfactory explanation to his question, "closer observation will confirm the Korean Air

Force has already been grounded by the same force that was originally used to neutralize the world's electricity back in 1951. The spacecraft could be generating an electrical interference or dampening effect within its immediate environment. As far as I know, there is no limit to the power the alien spacecraft is able to generate. Their technology is far beyond our abilities to comprehend."

"That's preposterous!" bellowed the chairman of the Joint Chiefs of Staff as he sprang to his feet, fists clenched and mouth working.

"Is that a careful and conscientious response, one borne of cold logic?" I asked, my voice growling with anger, the words coming slowly, painfully. "In light of what we have just witnessed, I do not believe there is much of anything that Gort or his spaceship are not capable of doing. Perhaps the CIA director can get us a verification through any remaining ground station operatives we have inside North Korea."

"Why isn't America's electricity neutralized . . . as you put it," asked the vice president in a more subdued manner as he shut his eyes and scratched the side of his head.

"I believe the spacecraft possesses the necessary technology and ability to localize the neutralization process to any specific area it so chooses. What I would like to know . . ." my voice trailed off slowly, as I became distracted by my thoughts, "is there anyone else inside that spacecraft? Is there some intelligent presence inside the spaceship directing the robot's actions? Mr. President, I have a very disturbing and sinking suspicion, a fear as it were, the robot has been programmed to carry out this mission of destruction from afar . . . that there is no other being aboard the spaceship directing his actions. If my observation is correct, we are not going to be allowed or permitted . . . a chance to intercede on our own behalf. If we are unable to defend our own ignorant actions to some higher authority within the spacecraft . . . if that supposition is true . . . then, gentlemen and ladies, we are doomed. For, no amount of begging or pleading will deter the robot from the inevitable completion of its mission on Earth."

"Excuse me, Doctor," the President of the United States interjected, his eyes luminous with anxiety and emotion, "it seems you have been able to form a working hypothesis as to the robot, its possible vulnerabilities, and the exactness of its mission?"

"Mr. President, I shall restate my observation and opinion that Gort has been programmed to destroy all nuclear related activities of every country possessing nuclear weapons. Reactors, research and development facilities, enrichment sites, power plants, and all strategic nuclear weapons and their accompanying operation centers will eventually face complete annihilation. It is my fear as well that any major city or industrial complex, along with the immediate surrounding areas, will also suffer complete and utter annihilation.

Gort has been programmed not terminate his actions on our planet until the possibility of all Earth's governments possessing nuclear-related facilities is completely and totally destroyed. As I have also stated before, we were warned and we failed to heed the warning. Now, it looks like we are going to pay a price too terrible to imagine for our willful and arrogant disobedience. Whatever powers sent Klaatu and Gort to Earth originally in 1951 have most assuredly decided to execute the balance of their threat. Of that, Mr. President, I have no doubt."

"Mr. President," the director of the CIA called out, whirling in his chair in a moderately excitable manner, "information from some of our sources in and around North Korea has been slowly filtering into our intelligence gathering centers in our Far East network. It seems Dr. Benson's theories and calculations may have been correct. Early reports indicate all electricity has been neutralized throughout the whole of North Korea, with some residual effect in the northern regions of South Korea as well. Aircraft cannot fly in the localized areas of the dampening effect, so this has effectively grounded the North Korean Air Force. However, interestingly, the nearby countries of Japan, China, and western Russia were unaffected by the neutralization process. This, apparently, was a highly specialized and localized event. Our scientists have stated the power necessary to perform such a feat is quite unimaginable. Quite impossible for our technology."

"The spaceship is moving again!" cried out the vice president as he pointed to the complex of monitoring screens within the room. I could feel the tension rise within the room as the spaceship began its routine of pulsating lights emerging from underneath the spaceship, which seem to always precede liftoff.

Everyone in the closed confines of the situation room simultaneously turned their attention toward the monitors. We could do nothing but watch silently, in fascinating horror, as the spaceship departed the area. The spaceship ultimately made its way toward the uranium enrichment sites located within the North Korean cities of Pakch'on, Ta'echon, Ch'onma-son. The ship would then travel farther north to the city of Yongjo-ri.

The terrible scene of destruction and desolation that accompanied the landing at each new site was to be played out over and over again with all nuclear-related facilities. Also, the Kumho Light-water reactor site and the Hamburg University of Chemical Industry were decimated, its crew vaporized in a matter of seconds. Each nearby city suffered the same savage and terrible fate until the result was the same immeasurable desolation. Every uranium enrichment site experienced the same manner and method of destruction as that which befell Yongbyon and Pyongyang. It was only a bit later when the full intelligence reports began to filter in that we realized the Pyongsong College of Science, the Kimchaek University of Technology, and the Kim Il

Sung University were also destroyed. In less than two hours, the country of North Korea was eliminated from the world's list of nuclear powers.

The cost in human lives was too horrible to imagine and could not be immediately calculated. I was astonished at how little effort was expended by the robot. Gort destroyed in one single, continuous movement. The ferocity of how it destroyed in so unequivocal a manner all things that lay in its path was intensely horrifying. There was no possibility of resistance allowed to the North Korean government and its defense forces. Their facilities were decimated, its people destroyed, and the country effectively plunged back into the Dark Ages. No electrical power, no modes of transportation . . . nothing of a modern nature survived. All regions remained eerily silent where the robot had been.

"My god," reiterated the president. "North Korea completely destroyed in less than two hours. I never thought I would live to see the day such tragedy would unfold before my eyes. I guess, like most human beings, I had always supposed the people of the Earth would ultimately be responsible for its own destruction. That we would end up destroying ourselves. Unbelievable. I want this spaceship and robot tracked. I want to know not only where it is headed next, but I want some kind trajectory plotted out concerning this spaceship's future movements."

"Well, Mr. President," I replied, as I pushed myself up from my seat, "my guess is the next target is likely to be . . . China!"

Chapter Four

China, Pakistan, India

1545
21 Dec 2012
Washington, D.C.

"Mr. President, you are going live on national TV in five . . . four . . . three . . . two . . . one . . ."

"My fellow Americans, this will be a national broadcast unlike any other president before me has had the unfortunate necessity to make. Doubtlessly, you all have heard rumors and reports of the utterly horrific and unbelievable events, which have transpired on our planet in the past forty-eight hours. These reports are true. A malevolent and apparently unstoppable extraterrestrial force has intruded into our lives, landing on our planet in the country of North Korea. Its hostile intentions were made appallingly clear when it initially destroyed our intelligence satellites, the space station, and then attacked our deep space center at the Cheyenne Mountain Complex. Subsequently, within the mere space of a few short hours after landing, North Korea had ceased to exist.

An evil, malevolent robot by the name of Gort has ostensibly begun a systematically planned destruction of some or all of the nuclear powers of the Earth. The full intentions of this robot and his mission on Earth still remain unclear at this time. The ominous extent of the robot's capabilities and powers has, unfortunately, been made crystal clear. What is known and what I can share with you tonight is that this spaceship and its robot have wreaked destruction on the countries of Korea and China, and is presently attacking the region of India and Pakistan. The destruction of Korea and China has been methodical and dreadful in nature, and completely without compassion or mercy.

At this time, Gort seems to be indestructible . . . the ultimate killing machine. All offensive actions to halt this wanton destruction and devastation of the Earth by this evil intruder have failed. While seemingly attacking only nuclear facilities, the collateral damage has been extensive. Whole thriving cities, with large populations of people, have been destroyed. While the death toll continues to climb, it must almost assuredly be in the tens of millions of people by now. There have been very few wounded and very few survivors from within the affected areas. I have expressed to the leadership of those countries attacked the American people's heartfelt thoughts and prayers. To those people affected by this robot's willful destruction of their homes and their loved ones, I can only say how very sorry we are for their loss.

My fellow Americans, the larger question facing us at this time is, how do we stop the unstoppable? How do we prevent a similar fate from inevitably befalling our country? You may rest assured that your government, with all its military might and capabilities, will do everything in its power to protect the United States of America . . . and the lives of every single American man, woman, and child. We will use every means at our disposal to destroy this menace before it reaches our shores. As always, Americans will unite and stand firm against this threat to our homeland . . . to our country we hold so dear to our hearts. And so, we task every American tonight to stay calm, do not panic. We will get through this. We will survive. Our country is and shall remain the greatest on Earth. I ask each of you to remain in touch with your local government agencies and the emergency broadcast network for further reports and updates. To the American people, I say thank you and God bless America!"

It was a bleak and dreary, somber situation room. As we all listened to the president's speech, everyone was lost in his or her own quiet observations. Although there seemed to be little time for reflection, we all waited breathlessly, watching the destruction of facilities and cities being played out upon our screens and monitors. I was later informed the president's speech to the American people seemed to have the momentary desired effect. As of yet, people may have certainly been worried, but not too terribly panicked. My guess was they were extremely hopeful that American military action would successfully stop the robot. I, on the other hand, held no such delusions about our ability to destroy Gort. I had witnessed the robot's awesome powers once before, and the sight had stayed with me always. At this particular time, gloom and desolation were the deeper and darker themes running through my mind.

We did not have long to wait for the president to rejoin the team waiting in the situation room following his address to the American people. Escorted by his secret service agents, he briskly entered the room, proceeding directly to his chair. There was a small smattering of applause from the group in appreciation toward his speech. With perfect and polite willingness, the president accepted the applause with a slight smile and a nod of his head to the group. Quickly reaching his seat, he sat down at the head of the large conference table. Abiding by the president's gesture, everyone else resumed their seats. All eyes were on the president. The room was essentially silent.

"What's the latest update?" he asked to no one in particular. The director of the CIA spoke first.

"Our intelligence sources indicate that the destruction of China's nuclear facilities and all related nuclear organizations has been completed. The Beijing Institute of Nuclear engineering and all of its surrounding buildings and complexes, along with Hua Fa nuclear plant, the China Institute of Atomic Energy, the China Nuclear Engineering Corporation, and even the Chinese Nuclear Society, which promotes relations between scientists, engineers, and organizations existing outside of their country, have been decimated. Nuclear institutes and organizations in the provinces of Qinshan, Shanghai, Shenzhen, Sichuan, Tianjin, Xian, and all of Southern China have been destroyed. There have been many other cities with nuclear power plants, organizations, and facilities that have been destroyed, which are too numerous to mention. China has virtually ceased to exist as a nuclear power or as a threat to any country of the world. As a leading nation in the world, it is finished. Apparently, all government buildings have been destroyed.

"Initial reports indicate casualties are approaching a billion dead. Secondary reports from our ground sources in China state that there, remarkably, is no stench of death, as in natural disasters. There is no outward manifestation of life in the affected areas. The robot has been absolutely thorough in its killing. No dead and decaying bodies. Virtually no wounded. The robot and spaceship have since relentlessly moved on to attack and destroy several nuclear facilities in India, including the Nangal Heavy Water Plant, the Rajasthan Atomic Power Station, and the Bharat Heavy Electrical Limited facility in New Delhi. The spaceship is currently located at the Narora Atomic Power Station. At the robot's present rate of destruction, we estimate it will have completely devastated India as a country within approximately one and a half hours. Worldwide casualties are currently estimated to be approaching the one billion mark."

"My god," muttered the President as he buried his head in his hands. "Have we had any word from within China?"

"None," answered the CIA director, his eyes fixed and motionless. He sat cold and waxen.

"Do we have a projected path of the robot?"

"My guess, Mr. President," I said slowly, taking all possible variables into consideration, "is that, quite possibly, Pakistan is next. After Pakistan, there exist a myriad of courses the spaceship could take. At this time, to offer a projected path of future destruction would be impossible."

"How the hell do we stop this thing?" asked the president abruptly, pounding his fist on the table to underscore his frustration.

"Mr. President, may I suggest . . . well, sir, we may not want to do anything just yet," the secretary of Defense chimed in uneasily. He licked his lips, closed his eyes momentarily, and adjusted his glasses. He cleared his throat and continued, "If everyone will stop a moment and analyze the situation calmly, I would point out that this robot has done nothing but annihilated the countries of our most hated enemies. The robot has, in effect, eliminated the nuclear threat of some of the most terroristic countries in the world! I think I understand what Dr. Benson is getting at along the lines of a possible sequence of events. But given any plausible sequence of events, if the robot continues, even remotely, on any of those suggested trajectories, the present course of action will most likely result in destroying the nuclear capabilities of the Soviet Union, Iran, and Syria. By the time the robot finishes path of destruction in Asia, the Middle East, and the European continent in general, the United States of America will stand alone in the world as the supreme power! The only nuclear power. Once those sequence of events occur, then we hit this robot with everything we've got!"

"That's monstrous!" I exclaimed aloud as I sprang up from my seat. "How can you even think—"

"Mr. President"—I was cut off by the secretary of Defense in a loud and powerful voice—"all I am suggesting is we wait and weigh all of our options carefully. Now is not the time for rash reactions toward something we know very little about. Even our foremost expert on the robot, Dr. Benson, has not offered any type of plan as to how to destroy this malevolent force ravaging our planet. The last thing we should do is strike without knowing more about our enemy . . . without knowing what kind of armed response would give us the best chance of success. I am sure even Dr. Benson would have to agree with my assessment. We cannot and should not strike until we have a proper amount of data and information concerning our enemy."

"Mr. President," the booming voice belonged to the chairman of the Joint Chiefs of Staff, "I must agree with the secretary of Defense. To attack this thing prematurely could be a grave and costly mistake. As far as we can tell, no one has been able to even scramble a single fighter jet against the invader. All attempts to attack with nuclear-tipped missiles have been repelled. Armies and air forces cannot advance against the threat. Both the robot and this damn spaceship seem indestructible. Mr. President, please do not misunderstand what I am saying. I am definitely not saying this robot and this ship cannot be destroyed. All I am saying is we had better be damn sure of what our concerted efforts and actions against this threat should be. All of our intelligence reports indicate we will not get more than one shot at this thing."

The president seem to seriously consider all that was presented to him. His thin lips compressed for a moment. Scratching the side of his head, he slowly moved his hand to his chin. He gave a little cough as if to clear his throat then spoke.

"Gentleman, I am not unaware of the advantages presented to the United States at this juncture in time. With how events have unfolded, and where the events have transpired before us, I would be clearly remiss in my duties as president and commander in chief if I did not take the necessary time to hear all possible courses of action against this threat. Perhaps a more methodical investigation into these events is warranted. As the general stated, in reality, we may only get one good shot at destroying the robot and the spaceship. Therefore, I believe we certainly cannot afford to squander or waste any opportunities toward that end. I am open to any and all options at this time. Dr. Benson, do you have any idea on how to stop this menace? Please, anything at all, no matter how ridiculous it sounds. This is the time for all available suggestions to be laid upon the table and discussed."

"Deprived of our ordinary resources of self-defense as we would appear to be, I think our only recourse of action is to try and communicate with Gort."

"What! That is preposterous!" simultaneously exclaimed the chairman of the Joint Chiefs of Staff and the secretary of Defense. Both men demonstrated a defiant scowl upon their faces. The secretary of Defense continued the attack. "How the hell do we even consider negotiating with something that is methodically destroying our planet? Since when do we lower ourselves to discussing anything with an enemy while combat operations are being waged? We have never done that."

"Bullshit!" I shouted back at the secretary as I felt my anger against him rising. I was not to be intimidated into silence now. "Just look at recent military history in the Iraq war. The U.S. Marines were halfway through the Battle of Fallujah, going after that radical Shite bastard Muqtada Al-Sadr and his group, and the Marines were kicking his ass too, I might add. Right in the middle of the battle, he cried out for negotiations because he knew he was in big trouble, and the piece of shit politicians stopped the attack and negotiated a truce! Right smack dab in the middle of a battle! Then he regroups, and he and his followers go on to kill many more Americans in the future. If you gutless leaders don't have the courage to do what is right militarily and not worry about far left radicals, the liberal politicians and the lawyers who write these ludicrous rules of engagement that put the lives of our troops at risk, then don't get in the damn war in the first place! Since we have adopted the lawyers definition of what war should be . . . these rules of engagement . . . we have never completed a military action successfully. And now, guess what Mr. Secretary? We got ourselves a war of total destruction. A war that we brought upon ourselves by not heeding the warning originally given to us back in 1951. We now find ourselves in a war against a force that will not be reasoned with, defeated militarily, or placated in any manner whatsoever, until this mission of destroying every country on Earth that possesses nuclear capabilities has been accomplished. The alien spaceship has the advanced technology to neutralize all the electricity in the world, and at the time of its own choosing. They possess the technology to eliminate all life on Earth, if that is their desire. This ability was efficiently demonstrated back in 1951 as well. We cannot begin to compete with their advanced technology. Nothing in our arsenal of defense is technologically capable of neutralizing the threat."

"But, Dr. Benson, as long as all of our cars are still moving, our planes are still flying and electricity is flowing smoothly, perhaps this power is not as great as you believe. Perhaps it is possible to successfully attack and neutralize the threat," said the secretary of State, forcing an irritable smile.

"My guess is in 1951, the electricity was only neutralized for thirty minutes simultaneously throughout the entire world due to the immense energy drain upon the ship's resources. To perform such a feat, the energy drain upon the alien ship must have been enormous. Since there is no need for such an enormous display or demonstration in this circumstance, and to minimize the energy loss on the ship's resources, a localized area of neutralization is all that is necessary. The rest of the world may have their power until it is their time to face destruction. The ship's energy source is undoubtedly vast, but not limitless. However, any device run electrically that comes into the sphere of influence of the dampening effect will be instantly affected. I would also like to take a moment to point out another supposition on my part. I am afraid we must also consider the possibility that the ship, given enough time, can somehow constantly regenerate power. So while the spaceship and robot's power may need time to regenerate, the same may not be true of the energy source. The source of energy may very well be limitless."

"Mr. President," the vice president commented acidly as his expression never changed, "let us not waste our time in any attempt to communicate with this robot. It must be destroyed! That is our only viable option! Communicating with an extraterrestrial robot sent to destroy us is not even possible. It should not be attempted, and it can't be done."

"On the contrary," I replied decisively, my voice becoming a little more strained, "my mother communicated a message to Gort. The message was given to her by Klaatu. The fact my mother was able to communicate with Gort probably saved the world. At the time she didn't know what the communication meant, but the meaning soon became obvious. Gort took her inside the spaceship, left her there alone, and exited the ship to bring back the body of Klaatu. Due to certain medical advances that, I'm sure, we still do not understand, Klaatu was brought back to life, and with no apparent residual injuries. Even though his gunshot wound was fatal! Now, I ask everyone assembled here today, how was the aforementioned accomplished except through communication? The world was saved by my mother through her communication with Gort back in 1951. I have no doubt of that. I believe communication with Gort is the only way we will survive this particular circumstance as well."

The secretary of Defense was about to jump back into the fray, but the president raised his hand in an abrupt manner and cut him off. After a distinct pause, the president stood up and addressed the assembled.

"Dr. Benson may be right. But the question remains, how do you intend to establish communication with Gort, Dr. Benson? It seems like anyone within a hundred miles of the robot ends up vaporized. And then there's the possible translation problem. We have no idea if the robot has been programmed to understand our language, and I am quite sure we don't understand his language. That is . . . if it even exists," stated the president with a bit of belligerent anxiety in his voice. I exhaled a deep breath, and responded in a subdued voice.

"Well, Mr. President, that is not exactly true. My mother was a very meticulous person. She kept a journal . . . a journal in which she wrote down every word she had personally heard spoken by Klaatu to Gort. This journal also contains the context in which those words were originally spoken. Just before she died, she gave me the journal. She made me vow to protect it with my very life. Apparently, she thought this day may come and believed her accumulated knowledge about the robot and the ship just might come in handy. It is a pity she didn't know just how right she would prove to be. Anyway, the journal is in a secure place in my home here in Washington. It is imperative I get ahold of that book immediately to begin research into mother's writings and recollections. With any luck, I may be able to piece together some rudimentary commands which can then be used on the robot's programming to halt this destruction."

"Mr. President!" The grim voice was that of the CIA director. "We are receiving some updates from India. The Uranium processing plant and the Uranium Corporation of India Limited have been destroyed, along with the Talcher Heavy Water Plant. Also, the Baroda Heavy Water Plant, the Hazira Heavy Water Plant, and the Kakrapa Atomic Power Station have been destroyed. All cities along with the surrounding areas have been vaporized. The robot has effectively neutralized the whole northern part of India! Latest reports have Gort proceeding toward the Tarapur Atomic Power Station. Strategic analysis states the logical path of nuclear facility annihilation would proceed as follows: the Mumbai Beryllium Machining Facility and collateral institutes, the Thal-Vaishet Heavy Water Plant, the Hyderdad Nuclear Fuels Complex, Special Materials Plant, the Uranium Fuel Assembly Plant, and all other nearby facilities in the immediate area. No notable resistance has been observed. Both the president and prime minister of India are sending out urgent appeals for help. We also continue to receive urgent requests from the peoples of North Korea and China. They are claiming a critical need for immediate aid . . . food, clothing, shelter, medical supplies, water . . ."

"Yes, I know," said the president as he slumped back down into his chair. "I am afraid there is not much we can do to offer help at this time. The sad fact of the matter is . . . we can neither help or send comfort and aid. With the electrical interference in effect around those areas, we couldn't get any supplies to the people. I'm afraid our hands are effectively tied at the moment. I met Prime Minister Rahji last year. He is a good man. A man of the people. He will do whatever is in his power to help the people of India. Send a communique to him stating our sincere condolences and voicing our regret that we cannot possibly send any aid at this time due to the overpowering nature of the threat. Let him know as soon as the threat has been neutralized, we will respond promptly and aggressively."

The situation room grew silent for a few seconds. Only the chatter of machines could be heard. An ugly expression had crossed the president's face, as he seemed to be fidgeting in his chair.

"Damn . . . as the head of the world's most powerful free nation, I never thought I would ever have to make a statement like that . . . to any head of government! This situation is damn near intolerable! Dr. Benson, retrieve your mother's journal, research it, and find a solution on how to communicate with this robot. God help us, that may be our only hope. As for the rest of you assembled in the situation room, I want a fully operational plan of attack against this extraterrestrial threat to our nation, and I want it in two hours. We must do everything in our power to halt this aggression against our world . . . at all costs, and preferably before it reaches our shore.

"Also, from Homeland Security, I want a complete evacuation plan for all major cities. I also want an evacuation plan for nuclear housing sites within our country. We must prepare to shut down and evacuate all nuclear facilities, that much is evident. Perhaps we can at least contain the damage if we cannot stop it altogether. Anyway, if we are unable to stop Gort, I want as many people given a chance to survive the future destruction as possible. Finally, we must prepare to move the seat of this government to the PEOC (The Presidential Emergency Operations Center) in the bunker below the White House, or to a secure, secondary location. I will be back in two hours to hear your reports. Dr. Benson?"

"Yes, Mr. President?"

"I want to personally thank you for attending this session, and for all your valuable insight. How long do you think you will need to piece together a preliminary report to me on your research?"

"Four to six hours, Mr. President," I replied with a bit of uncertainty in my voice. I had not seen the journal for years, and so I had no real idea what it may contain, or how helpful it may turn out to be."

"Make it four or less, Dr. Benson," the president replied with a resolute firmness in his voice as he rose quickly out of his seat.

Chapter Five

Research

1800
21 Dec 2012
Washington, D.C.

As I entered my mother's house, it was essentially as I had left it since the day of her death all those years ago. I readily admit it has cost me quite a lot of money to keep this house unoccupied all those years, especially with local and state governments running up the property tax bills as much as they had over time. Yet some curious feeling inside of me . . . told me there was a reason for doing so. I had never really figured out what that reason was until this day.

The house was a small two bedroom, two bath, with approximately 1200 square feet. As I opened the door cautiously, an unmistakable musty smell met my nose. The smell lingered throughout the house, denoting the ensuing years of non-use. I had maintained all the utilities for the house and found them to be working, so I promptly turned up the thermostat and put on a pot of coffee. Once I began to feel warm and human again, with a hot cup of coffee coursing through my veins, I knew it was time to begin my research of . . . the *book*. I gingerly retrieved the book from its secure location.

The first memory that struck me was what my mother, Helen, told me before she died. She impressed upon me that she had been very meticulous in recording every experience, every word, every nuance of all events transpiring on those fateful days so long ago. She had to be very careful about where she was recording, and what she was recording, as the full weight of the U.S. government was pressing down upon her. She stated she had endured frequent visits by the Secret Service, along with other government enforcement agencies.

Apparently, someone had leaked information as to what she was recording. The government officials, with startling rapidity, declared her writings a national security breach. She had been made to turn over to the government all keepsakes, mementos, and any other item at all in her possession that had anything to do with the spaceman Klaatu, his policeman robot Gort, or the spaceship itself. But Mother concealed the book well enough that the government could not get their dirty little hands on it.

The United States government could strip her of all her possessions pertaining to those events, but ultimately, they could not possess her memory. The fact that they could not completely destroy her mind might paradoxically end up being the very thing that saves this country. Everything . . . anything . . . she had written down could be the only existing key to stopping Gort. As I carefully began opening the book, I felt an involuntary shudder course through the entire length of my body. The fact struck me, oddly, that I had not seen or even thought about this book for almost forty years! Tears welled up in my eyes as a flood of memories raced through my mind. For a fleeting moment I found it most difficult to concentrate, even though I knew my ability to concentrate was to be of the utmost practical importance. I glanced nervously about and instantly felt sheepish that I had done so. I was quite alone and would be for the next few hours. The president had stated he would send a car to collect me at the appropriate time. Strict orders were subsequently issued I was not to be disturbed except under the most critical of emergencies.

As I found myself slowly sinking back into the comfortable lazy boy chair in the living room, I tenderly grasped the book. With great care, I brushed off the dust from the plain brown cover. I quite inexplicably began to feel an aroused state of anger course through my body. A torrential flood of memories concerning my mother's persecution by the government of the United States flowed through my tired mind. I hesitated a moment before reopening the book as I debated the thought whether this government deserved my help after all the harm they had caused my family. Did I really want to help our government out of this situation that they, and the other corrupt governments of the world, created? In seconds, I decided this government did not merit my help. However, the innocent lives of many Americans were at stake here as well. I reasoned I must act for their benefit, if for no other reason. So with a determined and resolute frame of mind, I opened the book.

The first page was blank, save for the name of my mother, Helen Benson. The second page contained a small table of contents. One below the other, the words: *Klaatu . . . Gort . . . Spaceship . . .* appeared. My mother had apparently split her observations into three distinct and separate categories. These categories were denoting the time spent with Klaatu, the time spent with Gort, and the time she had spent inside the spacecraft as well. I must confess, I was a bit indecisive as to where to start my research but finally reasoned the best place to begin was with the section labeled Gort. Stopping the robot's path of destruction was the paramount problem now facing our country.

In the space of a moment, I was staring at a full-page picture of Gort. Everything about that picture, from the robot's shiny, impenetrable metal alloy skin, to his general visage, sent a shudder of fear through my body. I hastily flipped the page in a wasted effort to erase that image from my mind. I was abruptly struck by the title of the next page: "Communication Spoken by Klaatu to Gort." Mother had written down not only the words spoken by the spaceman Klaatu to Gort but also the very context in which those words were uttered! This was almost more than I could have hoped for in any circumstance.

"God bless you, Mother," I said aloud with heartfelt conviction as I began reading what she had written. Tears clouded my vision.

The first words noted were spoken to Gort by Klaatu after Klaatu had been shot and wounded in the arm in his attempt to present to the world a gift of peace. The gift was a device that would have allowed our scientists to study other planets deep in our universe. The device was destroyed by the bullet, which then proceeded to enter the upper portion of Klaatu's left arm. The .30 caliber round exited the arm without striking a bone. After Klaatu had been shot and lay struggling on the ground, Gort had abruptly appeared at the pathway extending down to the ground from the base of the dome of the ship. The robot proceeded to slowly, deliberately, and with great purpose walk its way down toward the prone figure of Klaatu. Gort unexpectedly halted, raised his visor, and by the tactical use of the now-familiar white energy beam of high intensity light disintegrated some weaponry of the army. After seeing the destruction Gort had committed, Klaatu turned toward the robot and said, "Gort, *declanto rosco.*" These words had an immediate effect upon Gort. The robot suddenly lowered his visor and stood motionless.

These words had a chilling effect upon me. It stood to reason this find could be of singular importance! Perhaps this was the one command to Gort that would put an abrupt halt to any future carnage and devastation! But without a doubt, of equal importance and validity would be the question of whether the robot would recognize those exact words if I was the one stating them. Was Gort equipped with some type of voice recognition program? It seemed more than likely the robot could be programmed not to respond to any command while on his mission to Earth. Staggering under the visual imagery of me standing toe-to-toe with Gort, I momentarily wondered if I fully realized what I had gotten myself into? Every conceivable occurrence in confronting Gort should be deemed a possibility, but I reasoned I should worry about those aspects later. The first priority is to try and crack the language barrier. I drew an uneasy and deep breath, and refocused my attention on reading and absorbing.

Another command spoken by Klaatu to Gort, which my mother had written down, was the word *meringa.* Mother had noted that upon hearing the word *meringa*, Gort turned back toward the spaceship, proceeded up the walkway, and disappeared into the interior of the ship. *Meringa* thus must be reasoned to be a command to return to the ship. So perhaps those two phrases together . . . "Gort, *declanto rosco, meringa*," could not only effectively halt any impending destruction by the robot but also get him to return, to go back inside his spacecraft! My heart was beginning to beat faster. My mind raced to the insane and wild thoughts of commanding the robot! If only it were possible!

I quickly began to jot down some notes to myself then hurriedly continued on with my research. My efforts quickly came to an abrupt halt. The heading of the next section of the book sent a shiver down my spine that I could not suppress. I felt the hair on the nape of my neck stand up as I read . . . "Inside the Spaceship."

Mother had begun this section with a descriptive narrative of the inner compartments of the ship. She succinctly noted, once she was carried into the spaceship by Gort, she first observed an inner hallway that seem to circle the full circumference of the ship. There were no connecting seams or panels at all on the inner hull. It was as if the ship was perfectly molded into one set piece from the outset of its construction.

The floor of the outer corridor appeared to be made up of separate panels roughly three feet in width, which ran from the inner room wall to the inner hull of the ship. The height of the hallway seemed to be roughly ten feet, and the width was stated to be about the same. The material within the interior corridor seemed to be of the same type comprising the outside hull of the ship, as well as being the same type of metal alloy of which the robot seemed to be composed. The circular, inner passageway of the ship seemed to be amply lit, with light shining through what she described as some type of a slit-portioned wall. This also seemed to circle the circumference of the ship.

The immensity of the next few sentences were wholly beyond my powers of reasoning. An image of something very strange now caused me to shudder and draw a deep breath.

This astonishing and startling observation was that although the structure of the hull of the ship was of an impregnable metal alloy, she had very little trouble seeing through the metal hull of the ship! She could clearly observe the crowd that had later gathered for the meeting proposed by Professor Barnhardt! She calmly described the metal as being completely transparent from the vantage point of being inside of the ship! She had never spoken of this to me before she had died, so I found myself completely astounded by this revelation. A metal that was transparent from one side and impenetrable from the other! I shook my head as my thoughts raced on. I forced myself to continue my reading.

Mother's observations stated that once Gort had carried her across the circular hallway to the inner compartment of the ship, a door magically slid open where no door could be discerned previously. She quickly became aware of what seemed to her to be the spaceship's master control room.

Her artful renderings describing the inside of the main compartment were quite striking, and I paused a moment to scan her drawings. Once I had satisfied my curiosity, I continued with the reading.

Once the automatic door closed silently behind them, Mother noticed a set of five round lights on the metal frame of the door, and five lights on the frame of the adjacent wall where the door closed upon. Upon closing securely, the door and wall became seamless. The two rows of five lights now shone together as if they were one unit. Almost squarely in the center of the compartment was some type of large, active gyroscopic device in a Plexiglas dome covering. This was set atop a rather large round metal stand. The metal stand then securely rested upon a larger round metal base.

A shelf containing twelve small circular lights set equidistant from each other slanted downward from the base of the upper part of the circular container, extending to the top of the larger base. The shelf slanted downward for about two feet, and Mother estimated at about a ten-degree angle. The base at the Plexiglas dome was seemingly of a translucent material that either reflected light or produced light. She states she could not tell which. Various controls and different types of levers and switches could be seen in the interior walls under the transparent, plastic-dome glass.

Opposite one side of the gyroscopic structure was a rectangular, box-shaped, control panel that had many rows of lights and five Plexiglas cylindrical bars connecting to the base of the panel. Some type of circular clock-faced device was stationed directly above the control panel. Composed of the same type of plastic, and equidistant from each other, four cylindrical bars emanated from the outer ring of the device.

Directly to the left of the devices and connected both was a large circular screen. Upon the screen's face, Mother described what could be seen as a sort of large graph of squares. Within the graph, perfect circular lines existed, one larger than the next, emerging outward from the center of the screen. The smallest inner circle was bisected by two of the center graph lines, which made it ominously appear like a view from a rifle scope. Three lines arced up from one side of the bottom portion of the screen to the opposite side of the bottom portion of the screen. A small metal shelf connected the bottom of one control panel to an identical control panel on the other side of the huge screen. The screen was situated upon this shelf and was observed to run between the two control panels, effectively connecting all three of the devices. The same sort of circular clock-faced device also appeared above the opposite side control panel.

In the exact center of the ceiling of the chamber, directly above the Plexiglas gyro-type device, was a perfect circular hole about five to six feet in diameter, and at least three feet in depth, which apparently granted access to the upper dome of the saucer-type spaceship. Cut into the wall on the opposite side of the screen and control panels, was what can only be described as some type of bed or resting area. This was comprised of a rather uncomfortable-looking raised platform cut into the interior metal wall of the room. By Mother's account, it was seven feet long, four feet of which appeared to be cut into the side of the wall. There seemed to be some sort of crude metal pillow or headrest upon which one could lay one's head. This headrest curved up on either side of the head for about ten inches, which would adequately cover both sides of a person's head.

Directly behind the headrest was a small circular opening, and in front of the opening was a set of three circular, transparent tubes, which ran the full diameter of the opening. The bottom of the tubes lead directly into the headrest. The inside of the opening was clearly illuminated by an unknown and unseen light source. Extruding from the bottom center of the opening was a transparent plastic square positioned against the back of the wall inside the opening. From this square emanated a small transparent plastic tube fitting neatly into a transparent plastic box of about three inches, equal in length, width, and depth. This device would seem to be directly pointed to the center of the head when placed upon the headrest.

Mother had written that the previously described platform was the area where Gort had lain Klaatu down, eventually reviving him from the lethality of his wounds. At that time, the tube and box leading to the center of Klaatu's head was brightly illuminated. Once the procedure had been accomplished and Klaatu had risen from the dead, the inner circle, the tube, and the box became dark once again. Mother theorized this area was perhaps a sleep chamber and some sort of medic chamber as well.

Below her description and drawing of the inner chamber of the ship, a section of writing entitled "Screen Communication" appeared. Underneath this heading was a list of words or phrases she had heard Klaatu speak into the illuminated communication screen. Her interpretation of the words and phrases followed below the list. She writes in her book that Klaatu had wanted to speak with her briefly before contacting his planet and eventually exiting the spacecraft to address the assembled crowd. Here is the text of that conversation:

"Before I address Professor Barnhart and the assembled crowd, I will first provide a final report to the Association of Planets, whom I represent, regarding the status of my mission."

"What will you say to them?" asked my mother as she accompanied Klaatu to the large screen/communication device. Klaatu turned and faced her. Mother reports he spoke with unmistakable cold logic and without any trace of rancor.

"I can only report to them what I have honestly observed and come to believe about your planet. My report will state your planet is guided by governments that are run by small-minded individuals whose only object is to enrich themselves at the expense of others. That they have obtained the freedom to act irresponsibly with little or no effort or opposition from the people they govern. We had long watched your particular country, and I must say we were truly inspired and hopeful at its inauguration. But in the years since what you people call 'the revolution' has transpired, your country has begun to walk down that familiar path of bigger government, stronger government, more oppressive government. Individual freedoms were lost by your people as they were either too ignorant or too afraid to rise up against the government's increasingly oppressive policies. When any government obtains, permits, and enforces the policy of taking from those who earned it to giving it away to those who didn't, then that government has become corrupted beyond any reason. I do not know how, why, or when your countrymen lost the ability to accurately reason for themselves, but it will be painfully obvious to the Association of Planets that this has, indeed, occurred. I will therefore report the only reason your government exists, along with the rest of your planet's governments, is to extend its own life.

"Your government officials have lost the will and the capacity to care for and benefit the people they are sworn to serve. My report must necessarily include how all of your planet's leaders are acting immaturely and childishly and are not now, or in the foreseeable future, ready to join our association of planets. I will recommend one last chance for the people of your planet. I will address the assembled scientists and inform them of that last opportunity. If your governments fail to heed this last opportunity, and do not spurn and reject their violent tendencies, then I'm afraid there is no hope for the survival of your planet. Our Association of Planets will not permit one planet to jeopardize the safety of all other planets."

"What will happen to the Earth if our governments refuse to heed your warning?" my mother asked as she stood frozen, with a sudden sense of foreboding.

"Then Gort, or another robot similar to him, will be dispatched to this planet with the authority and power to turn your Earth into a burned-out cinder. I'm afraid this will be an irrevocable fate: complete and utter obliteration."

Mother states she almost collapsed at hearing the last part of Klaatu's statement, and sat down on a small ledge attached to the wall next to the large communication screen. She listened with great care and deliberation as Klaatu began his report, speaking directly into the illuminated communication screen. Mother committed to memory and later wrote down these words:

"Imray Klaatu narawak monkro bavall baratu lodensko implatit yobo terriaxal balenko buringi dingus."

It was this juncture in Klaatu's report to the Association of Planets that Mother reports there occurred a pause in the communications. She heard nothing for about a minute but noticed Klaatu was nodding his head slightly at several points, shrugging his shoulders indifferently. She reasoned that Klaatu must have been receiving some instructions or commands back from the Association of Planets, which were inaudible to her. During the entirety of this communication, Gort stood motionless against the far wall of the inner chamber. After a minute or so, Klaatu spoke again.

"Declaro orexicay ubo bosfor nowaki bixlo atalango candalli loto morata eckla boros kistoros pasloxo pilatto kuteka raymi okro."

At the conclusion of this report, Klaatu then waved his hands over a row of lights. This slight movement caused the lights to momentarily flicker then shut down. The illumination radiating out from the communication device also abruptly dimmed. Klaatu quickly turned toward Mother and offered a slight smile, then, without speaking a word, strode out of the main compartment. He returned to Mother in a short amount of time, dressed in his space suit, minus the helmet. Then, he and mother left the spaceship—Mother, to a life of derision and persecution and Klaatu, to address the assembly. Klaatu and Gort would then soon depart the Earth, their diplomatic mission at an end. The spaceship would then lift off from Earth and begin the long voyage home.

The final words Mother had translated, Klaatu had spoken to her while riding in the back seat of a taxi cab as they raced toward Dr. Barnhardt's house. My mother and Klaatu were desperately trying to arrive at Dr. Barnhardt's residence in an ill-fated attempt to succor safety for Klaatu until the time of the meeting. These words of obvious significance ultimately saved not only her life but the life of our people and our planet. It remains my belief this fact is absolutely unassailable. Those words spoken in the most urgent of tones by Klaatu were the words "Gort, Klaatu *Barada Nictoe.*"

Klaatu forced my mother to memorize those words in case the inevitable happened to him. She had been ordered to take all measures deemed necessary to deliver the message to Gort. Klaatu deemed it imperative for Mother to speak those words to the robot and firmly conveyed to my mother the terrible power embedded within the robot. If she failed to deliver the message, Gort could ultimately destroy the Earth. History records she was successful in her mission.

"Now, however," I thought ruefully as I closed my eyes tightly and nervously, "due to the illegal, unlawful, and immoral acts of the governments of Earth, Gort had now returned to finish what my mother had so decisively prevented in 1951."

I opened my eyes slowly and once again began to read. At the conclusion of Klaatu's speech to the assembled scientists of the world, Mother had returned home and immediately wrote down the spaceman's final warning. It used to be a well-known fact what transpired next. Gort, Klaatu, and mother had exited the spaceship. She walked down the ship's metal pathway to the ground and stood beside Professor Barnhardt. Gort stood motionless in close proximity to the upper portion of the ship, while Klaatu made his way down the sloping side of the ship. Klaatu moved toward the edge of the ship. This is where he stood tall, facing the assembly. There, he addressed the people of the Earth. The prophetic words spoken were later preserved and written down by my mother. Those words were as follows:

"I am leaving soon. And you will forgive me if I speak bluntly. The universe grows smaller every day. And the threat of aggression from any group, anywhere, can no longer be tolerated. There must be security for all, or no one is secure. Now, this does not mean giving up any freedom except the freedom to act irresponsibly. Your ancestors knew this when they made laws to govern themselves and hired policemen to enforce them. We, of the other planets, have long accepted this principle. We have an organization for the mutual protection of all planets and for the complete elimination of aggression. The test of any such higher authority is, of course, the police force that supports it. For our policeman, we created a race of robots. Their function is to patrol the planets in spaceships like this one and preserve the peace. In matters of aggression, we have given them absolute power over us. This power cannot be revoked. At the first sign of violence, they act automatically against the aggressor. The penalty for provoking their action is too terrible to risk. The result is . . . we live in peace, without arms or armies, secure in the knowledge that we are free from aggression and war, free to pursue more profitable enterprises. Now, we do not pretend to have achieved perfection. But we do have a system, and it works. I came here to give you these facts. It is no concern of ours how you run your own planet. But if you threaten to extend your violence, this Earth of yours will be reduced to a burned-out cinder. Your choice is simple. Join us and live in peace, or pursue your present course and face obliteration. We shall be waiting for your answer. The decision rests with you."

After a potent pause to emphasize and underscore his warning, Klaatu abruptly turned and walked back toward the interior of the spaceship. He stopped momentarily, turned to Gort, and spoke the last words he was ever to utter on Earth.

"Gort, *meringa*."

Then, Gort turned and, step by deliberate step, slowly disappeared into the spaceship. Klaatu gave a small wave, a certain wistful gesture of good-bye to my mother, and then abruptly turned and walked into the ship. The spaceship's walkway slid silently back into place as the dome's opening closed silently behind them. Again, no seam or breach could be discerned. Almost immediately upon Klaatu's disappearance into the spaceship, a faint but growing humming could be heard, and a pulsating glow from underneath the spaceship could be seen. As the glow and the hum increased in intensity, the assembled scientists began to scatter, to move as rapidly as possible away from the spaceship. The ship then gradually, almost leisurely, lifted off the Earth and disappeared with frightening velocity into the depths of deep space.

Our visitors of first contact were gone. It was not long after this that the governments of Earth colluded in their attempts to discourage anyone from speaking publicly about this event and to initiate a large publicity campaign to eradicate all evidence this event had ever happened. The huge pressure brought down upon my mother was unbearable. At first, the United States government placed my mother in "protected custody" while they debriefed her. I remembered the development vividly as I did not see my mother for weeks and was worried sick about her. Then, one day, quite unexpectedly, she returned home. She was not the same person she had been when she had left. Whatever it was they had done to her, whatever method of debriefing was utilized, the treatment had aged her significantly. It was as if they had broken her spirit, for I did not ever see her smile or laugh again. She seemed to only be a shell of her former self, almost lifeless. I cried for weeks after her return. It was only a few years later she died.

I wiped a tear from my eye as I made a determined effort to halt those tormenting memories. I returned my attention to the book. It seemed as though some of the words would be easily translated. For instance, the word *meringa* apparently could be loosely translated as "come" or "come back inside the ship." Other words and phrases would be harder, perhaps impossible to translate. However, the phrase that drew my attention over and over again, was the phrase, "Gort, *declanto rosco*." These words were the phrase that stopped Gort's initial rampage in 1951. The robot instantly shut down and remained motionless until activated by Klaatu at a later time.

Also, one could reasonably argue and assume the phrase "Gort, Klaatu *barada nicto*" must have meant something along the lines of "Gort, find Klaatu, bring him back to the ship, and use all means and powers of the ship to resuscitate, revive, or resurrect him from the land of the dead." For some reason, this phrase seemed to strike me as being extremely important as well, but I would not know how much so until later, when it would effectively save my life.

The most difficult phrases to translate would be the words or phrases Klaatu used in communicating to his home system of planets. There would be practically no point of reference upon which to infer or extrapolate much of anything. I believed our only hope of deciphering any information from Klaatu's report to the home system of planets, would be the use of the government's ultrasophisticated translation computers. These were located within the veil of secrecy surrounding the Central Intelligence Agency headquarters in Arlington, Virginia.

There was, however, the initial portion of Klaatu's report that I could, with some degree of certainty, decipher and interpret. My mother's writings indicated Klaatu had always started his reports with the words *"Imray* Klaatu." I permitted myself a small chuckle as I thought "it would definitely not take an individual of sharp, analytical ability to translate the phrase into "This is Klaatu reporting." The rest of the words in the report would be a great deal harder to decipher.

At this point, I must confess to being overwhelmed with enormous doubts that we could translate any portion of the transcripts since this language was not based on any form of earthly language.

"Our computers would have to start from scratch and try to find some type of—"

My thoughts were unexpectedly interrupted by a loud, curt series of raps upon the outer door of the house. I managed a quick glance at my watch as I arose from the comfortable confines of my chair. I was startled and amazed that a time period of three and a half hours had elapsed. It seemed like only minutes earlier I had sunk down in the chair, becoming thoroughly engrossed in my mother's writings. As tired as I found myself to be, it would not come as a complete surprise if I had even, at some point, dozed off during the process.

A thin, tall man in an air force officer's uniform greeted me as I hastily opened the front door. He stood about six feet, three inches tall, with a clean-cut face, and glinting eyes. The uniform he was wearing bore the insignia resembling railroad tracks. The captain's steady and discerning gaze immediately imparted the thought that he was a man on a mission, and not to be trifled with in the least. His expression never changed, as he spoke to me in an unfailingly courteous manner.

"Dr. Benson, I am here to provide you immediate transportation to the White House, sir. If you would please gather anything you need from your premises, we shall depart for the White House as rapidly as possible."

"Let me grab my coat and my research book and papers, and then I am all yours, Captain," I replied as I turned back into the interior of the house. The captain followed me into the room, not waiting for an invitation. It then dawned on me he probably had orders not to let me out of his sight for even a moment of time. I picked up my long, winter trench coat and put it on, then I grabbed my mother's book and my papers upon which I had scribbled some notes.

Turning to the captain, I stated, "I'm all yours, Captain. Shall we go?"

The officer silently followed me out of the house, closing and locking the door behind him. Parked directly in front of my house was a large black limousine, with its back door already open. Melodramatically, the open door seemed to be beckoning me to climb inside the vehicle. I closed the door and watched the captain walk around behind the limousine and get in the back seat next to me. As soon as the captain had entered and closed the door, the limousine began to move. I slowly, sadly, took one last, long look at the house I would be destined to never step foot in, or lay eyes upon, again. Gloom, desolation, and a deepening sense of despondency began to pervade my mind and body to the very depths of my soul. For the remainder of the short ride, I found I could not shake the feeling of doom and gloom. A storm of conflicting emotions raged within me, while a few drops of rain began pelting the windshield of our vehicle. The weather was beginning to match my mood very nicely.

Chapter Six

Back in the Fire

2345
21 Dec 2012
Washington, D.C.

As I sluggishly exited the comfortable interior of the limousine, the very first face I noticed was that of the White House chief of staff. He was standing with arms clasped in front of his waist. He looked a lot like I felt . . . tired and haggard. As I closed the door of the vehicle behind me, I noticed he had maintained a dead silence.

"Now what?" I thought to myself.

The gloomy and dreary atmosphere of the president's personal, secret underground garage, seemed to weigh even more heavily upon me. As I afforded myself a quick glance around, I could see the president's designated limousine in a small row of other black-colored limousines. A more meticulous investigation of the underground garage probably would have been conducted, in order to satisfy my natural curiosity, but at this moment, I was just too fatigued to even think about it. The White House chief of staff approached me with his right arm and hand extended. After I warmly shook his hand, he gestured toward what appeared to be an elevator door that had just opened. He did not speak a word until we both were secure inside the luxuriously decorated lift. As we began to ascend, he deliberately turned toward me and spoke in a hushed voice. It was almost a whisper.

"I hope you have had some luck, Dr. Benson, because we sure as hell haven't."

"Oh no! Don't tell me. Let me guess. You ran out of ravioli?" I asked, with an evident, nervous laughter. I was simultaneously wanting to get an update on events but, also, dreading what I feared I would hear. During the limousine ride, the captain and I had maintained an eerie, almost impenetrable silence. The captain's determined silence meant the gratification of my curiosity would have to come later. Apparently, the time had come. For the most part, Scott ignored my jest.

"The robot seems unstoppable," he replied glumly as the elevator ground to a slow, almost imperceptible halt. In a few more moments, the doors had silently opened and we both exited the elevator together. Scott began to steer me in the desired direction as we continued our conversation.

"When you left the White House to attend to your research, India was in the process of being decimated. The robot made short work of every nuclear facility in India. Estimates of casualties in India are topping 250 million, with very few reported as being wounded. It goes without saying India has been devastated. We still have reports coming in from that country, and with each report, the casualty figures grow. Casualties could end up being over 750 million. We just don't know yet. In concluding the work in India, the robot then turned its attention to Pakistan. Dr. Benson, Pakistan used to have a population of around 175 million. The robot's first target was the Kahuta Khan Research Laboratory where their large-scale uranium enrichment centrifuge was located. Our most recent intelligence reports indicated this plant used to produce weapons-grade uranium for Pakistan's nuclear devices. Nothing exists there now but a pile of molten metal. Islamabad and surrounding areas up to a hundred-mile radius are also completely destroyed. For your information, Dr. Benson, Islamabad was where their nuclear weapons assembly plants were located, along with their nuclear research and development sites. All of their plutonium extraction sites have been leveled. Everything from the cities of Golra and Wah in the north to Lahore in central-east Pakistan have been decimated. Heavy water reactors, plutonium production reactors, nuclear power reactors no longer exist in Pakistan. Destruction was complete all the way down the country to Karachi in south Pakistan. Even the 1998 nuclear test sites in Ros Koh, in the Kharan Desert in east Pakistan were targeted. Our intelligence sources indicate an estimate of at least 100 million dead. An interesting observation out of all this is the robot seems to have the ability to fire in small patterns or to create a large swath of destruction stretching for miles. I think everyone now agrees with your assumption the robot is targeting nuclear facilities and seats of government. Anyway, Pakistan has virtually ceased to exist as a country . . . much the same as India, China, and North Korea."

"My god," I uttered almost imperceptibly as we rounded a corner and headed toward a set of doors at the end of a long hallway. The robot was destroying countries at an inconceivable speed. I was about to speak when Scott continued his small brief of the current situation.

"I'm afraid, Dr. Benson, the destruction in India and Pakistan is just the start. After destroying Pakistan, Gort turned his attack toward Iran. We first started receiving reports of attacks on the Saghand, Yazd Province, where most of the uranium mining occurs in Iran . . . seven thousand tons of uranium reserve effectively destroyed. The United States and Israel in a combined attack couldn't have done a better job of it! Then Bushehr was attacked. This was the site of their light-water reactor, with the fuel being supplied by Russia, of course. The site was totally destroyed in a matter of moments. The entire area looked as desolate as the moon's surface after the attack. The Nuclear Research Center in Isfahan was next. This was the Iranian's uranium conversion facility containing four known reactors. This was shortly followed by the destruction of the heavy water production plant at Arak; the pilot fuel enrichment plant where their 164-centrifuge cascade was installed and operating. These attacks were shortly followed by an attack on the pilot laser enrichment plant in Lashkar Ab'ad, which the Iranians swore was shut down and dismantled in 2003. Guess they weren't exactly telling the truth on that one."

"When have they ever told the truth about anything?" I asked as I snorted in disgust.

"Finally, the total destruction of Tehran was accomplished. Tehran is where the Iranians had their primary nuclear research center containing their light water, HEU, research reactor. The barracks of the Iranian revolutionary guard was also obliterated. No tears shed for that one," the White House chief of staff continued with a wry smile, deftly ignoring my interjection. "The CIA's latest intelligence indicated that within the city of Tehran was also where their uranium conversion experiments were conducted. Also, the Kalaye Electric company was situated in downtown Tehran, which was a primary site of all their centrifuge testing. Every single government building was also targeted and eliminated. The entire thriving city has been wiped out. There were also a few other sites that the robot attacked and destroyed. However, we had no actionable intelligence on those sites. Anyway, total destruction and devastation was completed within approximately forty-five minutes of Gort's initial assault. The robot is moving with a swift and terrible sword."

We had reached the end of the hallway. Scott opened the door leading into a small anteroom chamber. A row of small and beautifully upholstered Victorian-era chairs lined the wall on the right side of the set of double doors. Above the chairs were two framed pictures, one of President Washington and one of President Lincoln. Scott gestured for me to have a seat in one of the chairs. As I did so, I could not help but wonder, as I stared at the portraits of Presidents Washington and Lincoln, just how far we have slipped in the quality of man the American people elect as their president. I shook my head sadly. If only we Americans had not allowed elections to degenerate into the irreprehensible act of electing the best politician money could buy.

"If you will wait here a moment, Dr. Benson, I will let the president know you have returned," the White House chief of staff stated as he gave a slight rap upon the door. Slowly and deliberately he opened the door and stepped into the next room.

I surmised I was sitting, once again, outside the president's situation room. There must be a few of these anterooms connecting to the larger situation room, as this one was quite different than the last one in which I had found myself waiting. This particular room seemed to be more austere than the previous room. The last waiting room had been ornately decorated with all manner of furnishings. I was abruptly shook out of my restless thoughts as one of the double doors opened slightly. Leaning his head and shoulders out of the opening, Scott silently motioned me to get up and follow him through the door and into the next room.

As I entered, I immediately recognized the familiar layout of the president's situation room. The president was sitting as still as stone in his reserved seat at the table, as were all the president's advisors. Everyone seemed almost in the identical position as when I had left them about four hours ago. As soon as he saw me, the president sprang up from his seat. The room suddenly became hushed and expectant. He came around the end of the conference table to meet me and seemed as if he was grateful to have me back in his presence. My eyes widened in astonishment as he shook my hand a little too vigorously. He put his other hand on my shoulder and proceeded to escort me to my seat. As we walked toward our seats, he spoke in a solemn, but curious tone of voice.

"I guess Scotty has been bringing you up to date on what has been happening in the world?"

"Yes, Mr. President. I understand India, Pakistan, and Iran have been attacked and decimated within the past couple of hours. Exactly where is Gort now?" I asked as he left me at my seat and proceeded toward his own place at the conference table. I slumped down wearily into the softness of my executive-style chair as I awaited the president's answer. His eyes flickered nervously under raised eyebrows.

"The robot is currently in central Russia. The Russians have been attempting to attack and destroy the robot but have failed miserably. It seems nothing electrical in nature can be used effectively in any manner against the technologically superior defensive array of the robot. Both ship and the robot are impervious to any type of attack mounted against them thus far. We have received intelligence reports from our operatives within the Soviet Union. These reports estimate the Russians have lost more than half of their fighting forces against the robot. In point of fact, our last intelligence reports stated the Russians were using horses in an antiquated cavalry charge in an effort to get their troops close to the robot. Unfortunately, they were wiped out to the man. So many brave men . . ."

The president paused momentarily, shaking his head heavily. His gaze was steady and cold as he continued, "From these preliminary intelligence reports, we have also been able to observe that the robot began his attack in far eastern Russia. The Petropavlovsk nuclear submarine pens were obliterated, followed in rapid succession by Komsomolsk-Na-Amure nuclear submarine pens, the Sovetskaya Gavan nuclear submarine pens, the Primorye submarine pens at Vladamir bay, along with the Nakhodka submarine pens just east of Vladivostok. The nuclear rocket facility at Arsenyev was also destroyed along with the heavy bomber base at Ukrainka.

Other nuclear-related sites destroyed in east Russia include the facilities within the cities of Yuzho-Sakhalinsk, Khabarovsk, Birobidzhan, Blagoveshchensk, Magadan, Palana Anadyr, the nuclear reactor site at Bilibino . . . hell, they are just too numerous too mention," stated the president as he threw down the list from which he was reading in a most disgusted manner, angry he was forced into merely pitiful observation. He continued in a clear, testy voice.

"Another bit of interesting news was the robot wasn't within three hundred miles of some of those locations when they were disintegrated by some energy beam. We have evidence, coming in, the spaceship is also programmed to carry out attacks independently of the robot. Now we have two sources of destruction occurring simultaneously! Our last intelligence reports indicate the robot seems to be headed toward Moscow, destroying everything and everyone in its path. In every circumstance, there is no reasonable expectation of survivors. Dr. Benson, I sure as hell hope you were successful in your research on discovering a way to stop this ungodly thing, because once the robot deals with Israel, France, Germany, and Britain, it's going to be headed our way."

The president paused momentarily and pointed at the images on the screen.

"Evidence by the rapidity of his progress in destroying the known world, our best estimate is the robot will be at America's doorstep in approximately six hours. It's damn near one o'clock in the morning, so that means we are expecting Gort at approximately seven in the morning on our East Coast. We have been busting our brains through the night trying to figure out a way to stop this wanton destruction. We have not, as of yet, come up with any offensive operation that is even remotely possible of being pulled off successfully. When aircraft won't fly, bombs won't explode, and weapons will not fire due to this electrical dampening effect, what the hell else is left? Shall we throw sticks and stones at it? Use bows and arrows?"

The president slumped back down into his chair and stared straight at me. He struck me as a defeated, gaunt, unhappy-looking person, weighed down by the weight of the world upon his shoulders. For the first time in what seems like ages, I felt a small but growing measure of sympathy for a politician and one of the world's leaders.

Due to the collapse of the dollar in late 2010, the USA had slipped dramatically among the world's players. However, we were still a recognized and somewhat respected nation in the eyes of most of the world. And the president, as the leader of the nation, was now cast back in the spotlight. It seems the eyes of the world were once again focused upon our country. Throughout history, when natural disasters struck any country, the United States of America was always the first and foremost to offer aid and hope. Indeed, it seems every time the world is in some sort of crisis, all eyes turn toward the United States to come up with a plan to deal with that crisis. Before I could speak, the director of the CIA suddenly interrupted.

"Mr. President, we are receiving reports that the robot has destroyed all related nuclear facilities in the cities of Irkutsk, Bratsk, Novosibirsk, Omsk, Nizhnevartovsk, along with all structures in and around those cities. Devastation stretches for thousands of miles. The robot is currently approaching the Ural mountain range at an incredible pace. Our Russian colleagues, the KGB, are stating that they have inflicted damage upon the robot but refuse to issue specifics. I don't think those reports are true. There is no reliable evidence to indicate anything has slowed the robot at all.

"The Russian Military of Defense has since issued a statement that they are massing their remaining forces to intercept the spaceship at the Ural mountain range. They have also issued an evacuation order to all nuclear warheads research and development laboratories, fissile material production facilities, serial warhead production facilities, and testing sites. The Ministry of Atomic Energy in Moscow is evacuating their buildings as well. Also, an emergency evacuation order to all citizens of Moscow has been instituted. Mass panic is being reported in Moscow . . . widespread looting and pillaging . . . and . . ."

"Thank you. I think we get the picture," replied the president in a gesture of resignation and impatience.

The sort of ordered chaos within the room began again, as each department head was being briefed and updated by what seemed like several different sources on several different levels of communication devices. Telephones, radios, computers were all being used simultaneously. It seemed to me the room was possessed of nightmarish reality.

"Dr. Benson," the president said with a smile that seemed cold and heartless. He began to fidget restlessly in his rather oversized chair. "I am forced by circumstance to agree with your previous logic that no military force can oppose this technologically advanced robot. Therefore, I believe our only hope lies with what your research has uncovered and developed. I am hereby giving the standing order that all of our technology be placed at your disposal. What can we do to help?"

I was at once shocked and taken aback by the nature of the president's statement. The words quivered in my brain. As I surveyed the room, I could observe raised eyebrows and glances being quickly exchanged among the president's inner circle. A disquiet again reigned within these confines. But for the moment, no one spoke. A profound silence was maintained. With a sense of calm expectation, I slowly raised myself up from my chair, simultaneously opening my mother's book and picking up the resultant research I had carefully placed between the pages. I was about to find myself transitioning out of the research stage and into the practical planning phase. Having had little time for reflection, I resolved to just speak and let the chips fall where they may.

"Mr. President, the fact that this planet was not destroyed in its entirety from a selected position from outer space leads me to draw a decisive and important conclusion. Although I do believe they have the technologically advanced weapons system to accomplish the destruction of our planet from the depths of space, the fact this was not executed or realized indicates to me that the ruling governments of the other planets, who sent this spaceship and robot to Earth, did not have the overt intention of completely annihilating our planet.

"Again, please believe me when I say that act could have easily been accomplished from a distance. Therefore, I must assume that Klaatu emphasized to his superiors that while the governments of the Earth were corrupt, hostile, and prejudiced, the people themselves were not altogether corrupted or evil. I believe Klaatu met many good people in his short stay on Earth, my mother being the most prominent among them. Although many human beings are prejudiced, easily excitable, and easily spurred on toward fearful and violent reactions, especially toward events of the unknown, Klaatu must have realized many human beings were more reasonable and rational than those he had contact with in the government."

I paused a few seconds to let the last statement sink in. Then I continued.

"I now offer the supposition that a means of our salvation may have been intentionally left open to us as a people . . . if we would only demonstrate the sanity and reason to find it. I must admit, although my research is just in the preliminary phases, and since we have precious little time to proceed, the final stages of a well-reasoned and workable plan toward halting the inevitable destruction of our country must be rapidly developed. Thanks to the efficiency of my mother's observations, my research indicates there is a phrase, which if processed and accepted by Gort, may have the desired effect of ending this threat."

"What!" exclaimed the secretary of Defense, in a resolute scowl of defiance and intractable ferocity. He had sprang abruptly to his feet, his eyebrows arching to underscore his indignation. "You are seriously going to stand there and tell me—"

"Excuse me, Mr. Secretary!" interrupted the president in a booming voice that seemed both tired and annoyed, "will you please give Dr. Benson the courtesy of being heard out?"

"Thank you, Mr. President. If there are no further interruptions, I will continue," I replied with my own gesture of impatience while staring at the secretary of Defense. I quickly looked around the situation room at the faces of those present. No one offered any further statements or outbursts. Everyone was staring at me with owlish eyes. As I stood grim and dismayed, I began my discourse once again.

"As I stated previously, I may have answer to the question of how we stop Gort. There are no guarantees it will work. There are no guarantees I can even get close enough to Gort to present the phrase without getting vaporized in the process."

I sat back down into my chair and continued.

"Thankfully, my mother kept a fairly extensive, comprehensive diary of all known communication between either Klaatu and Gort, or Klaatu and the Association of Planets. My mother was actually inside the ship's control room when Klaatu was reporting to his world. Mr. President," I said as I turned toward him, "it is essential these words and phrases be immediately analyzed by the most sophisticated translation computer available. If I am not mistaken, the CIA can help on this requirement."

"I will place at your disposal both the National Security Council and the CIA," responded the president in a decisive manner. Both representatives in attendance of the aforementioned organizations arose from their seats and walked uneasily toward me. With expressionless faces, both eyed the list suspiciously. Hesitantly, the director of the CIA took the papers from my hand. I found myself watching tensely as both individuals walked briskly out of the situation room. Even though there was a definite chill in the air, I moved on with dogged determination. I turned my attention once again to the president.

"Mr. President, if we are able to get some sort of accurate translation out of that list, it may be very helpful to our cause. However, I do feel it is prudent to proceed with the few words my mother and I have translated. I can state with considerable certainty that these words have an accurate meaning. According to my mother's recollections, the word *meringa* had been used twice with the robot. In both instances, the robot immediately turned around and entered back inside the spacecraft. We can theorize *meringa* is a command to return immediately to the spaceship. Whether the word can be part of a command employed to induce him to stop all his activities and get him back into the ship remains to be seen. But, Mr. President, it is a start."

The president's eyes widened at my last statement.

"Please, continue," stated the president flatly.

"This second item from my research is perhaps the most important. This phrase was spoken to Gort by Klaatu after Gort had come out from the spaceship to rescue Klaatu who had been shot and wounded by army personnel. The robot had used his destructive energy beam to eliminate weapons from the nearby proximity in an effort to protect the fallen Klaatu. The words Klaatu spoke to Gort were . . . *"declanto rosco."* Once these words had been spoken to the robot, Gort closed his visor and assumed a motionless position lasting for many hours. If I could somehow place myself within close proximity of Gort, hopefully without getting killed in the process, I may be able to communicate this phrase to him. If so, I may be able to elicit a favorable response. Hopefully, the robot would respond in much the same manner as with Klaatu issuing the command in 1951."

The president leaned forward, his elbows resting on the table. He now was acutely alert to every word and gesture.

"However," I continued as I drew a deep breath, "I must caution everyone that my theory does not and cannot cover all the possibilities. The robot may be programmed to only respond to a certain voice pattern. It may respond only to a certain frequency. It may be programmed not to respond to any outside stimulus. If this is the case, I will not survive. There is no guarantee, as I have stated previously, that this approach will work at all. However, I believe it is perhaps our best hope. Maybe the only hope we have. If I can get the robot to respond to these commands, we may be able to halt Gort's destructive progress. With a bit of extreme luck, I may even be able to get him back inside the ship and on his way home. Anyway, unless someone has a better idea, which, believe me, I would be more than happy to entertain, as I have no death wish to find myself face to face with Gort. Anyway, in my view, my plan is certainly worth a try."

"Mr. President"—the voice belonged to the secretary of Defense—"we are receiving reports the robot has crossed the Ural Mountain range and has simultaneously launched attacks against the cities of Perm and Izhevsk located on the Volga River."

I automatically turned to watch the screen as Gort, with raised visor, was commencing his attack, spreading the deadly, intense white light of his laserlike weapon. It was the same image. Where once thriving cities had stood, now existed only a molten pile of metal and ashes. In the mere space of seconds, a city disappeared and a desolate landscape appeared. Everyone caught in the beam of energy simply disappeared into nothingness. This absolute power used by the robot was a sight too horrible to behold. I felt I could actually observe the Earth shuddering under the terrific impact of the unbridled energy. The majestic appearance of the spaceship and the robot was immediately contrasted by the stupendous destruction of everything in its path, and the absolute human misery being perpetrated upon the masses of every country the robot had visited.

The situation room remained discreetly silent. The mounting sense of strain was magnified for a few minutes as all in attendance watched the terrible scene in a complete state of awe. As I watched in horrific fascination, I was struck by the thought that Gort did not stray very far from his spacecraft. Once his intended targets were destroyed, the robot would turn and reenter the spacecraft, making a short flight to his next target. It wasn't long until Gort was headed down the Volga River toward the city of Volgograd. The president broke the silence, speaking in a tone of voice that gave significant weight to every word.

"There is now nothing standing between the robot and the city of Moscow. There is no need to guess what has happened to the Russian forces amassed at the Ural Mountains. The robot moves with relentless determination. To militarily engage the robot seems suicidal at this point. Our early analysis of possible vulnerabilities of the spacecraft or the robot have yet to be proved adequate. In fact, appropriate analysis has been significantly less than we had hoped for. To be quite frank, our attempts to find any exploitable weak points has been an unmitigated failure."

"Mr. President, we are receiving reports . . . coming in . . . the Russian forces suffered 100 percent annihilation. No wounded . . ." stated the secretary of Defense as his voice trailed off as he finished reading his last statement. His face betrayed a perceptible sense of sad disbelief. Everyone continued to have their eyes riveted to the screen as the sight of Gort, moving with a deadly purpose toward its intended targets then obliterating those targets with a frightful velocity, was a detestable sight too horrible to turn away from. It was then that the director of Homeland Security, in a subdued voice, spoke slowly and deliberately. The urgency of the words spoken was quite unmistakable.

"Mr. President, I strongly suggest we commence an immediate evacuation of all major cities on the East Coast, especially those areas where we have nuclear reactors or any type of nuclear-related facilities. We should evacuate all unnecessary personnel to points of safety outside the targeted areas. I also recommend standing down our military and evacuating all military bases within the United States. I believe it has been more than amply demonstrated . . . any military force deployed against the robot would consequently face immediate annihilation. There can be no assured measure of success. If we stand down our military and disperse them accordingly, we will, perhaps, be the only one of the major powers having any type of military force remaining after the concluding assault. It is my opinion this is our most prudent course of action in the face of a complete, catastrophic failure against the robot. I believe, it would be the most prudent course in which to proceed and, ultimately, in the best interests of the United States. Mr. President, I request those orders to be issued immediately."

"Mr. President, that is completely ludicrous!" roared the voice of the senior military commander as he jumped to his feet. The general's thickset jaw was skewed in a look of intense ferocity and indignation. "Our forces are the best in the world, and they are ready as can be to face this . . . this . . . robot. My boys are licking their chops to have a go at this damn monstrosity. Damn it, Mr. President, what the hell are the American people going to think and say when their military turns its collective asses and runs like hell? We have to make a stand to protect our country!"

The general paused momentarily to allow his words the time necessary to have the proper effect. Then, he continued.

"It is readily apparent to me, and should be to everyone else in this room, that this thing is not only attacking and destroying military and nuclear targets, it is also destroying the seats of governments of those countries it has attacked! There is no effective government entities left in North Korea, China, India, Pakistan, Iran, and soon there will be nothing left of the communist government in Russia. No, Mr. President, our military forces cannot just sit idly by while this robot destroys our country. We must put up an aggressive counterattack against this threat. To not do so would most certainly damn us in front of the entire nation."

"Mr. President," the carefully restrained voice of the vice president said, eyes flickering as he joined the discussion, "I believe the general is correct. We must, at the very least, expend some type of an effort at militarily confronting the robot. It is my considered opinion the American people would never forget our surrender, our ultimate capitulation to this . . . menace. Mr. President, if you think our approval ratings are low now . . ."

"Approval ratings! Is that what the hell you're worried about?" I exclaimed vociferously as I arose from my seat. I calmed myself the best I could for a second then continued. "For the sake of your political ass, you are going to send our troops into an assault which would be final, decisive, and all-conquering . . . one that they would not be able to survive? All the assimilated data vehemently suggests conventional military forces are completely useless, helpless, and irrelevant against Gort. The robot will utterly annihilate them before they can even assume a position in striking range. All available scientific evidence indicates that even if you could set off a nuclear device right below his feet, there is no conclusive evidence it would even put a dent in the metallic substance of either the robot or the spaceship. It would be nothing short of suicidal to engage Gort militarily. Our only hope of salvation is to communicate with the robot in an attempt to reprogram it."

"Communicate with it? Hell, Mr. President, why don't we ask it over for dinner?" replied the general sarcastically as he turned toward the president. "Force only understands force. This robot cannot be reasoned with at all, if you ask me. The robot was sent here on a mission, and it will not return to where it came from until that specific mission is completed. Whoever it is that sent this robot here, programmed it to destroy our way of life on Earth. Whether the governments of Earth have done anything wrong or not is not the issue here. At least, not anymore. Survival is the issue. Survival is the only concept we need to worry about now. We'll have time to worry later about the reasons and motivations behind this assault on our planet. Mr. President, it is my opinion we must concentrate all of our forces on eliminating this threat."

"Mr. President," replied the vice president angrily through tightly drawn lips, "the only point I am trying to make is the American people expect their elected officials to do something in their defense. If we fail in that sacred task . . ."

"Thank you, everyone," stated the president in an abrupt manner as he rose from his seat, effectively ending all conversation. Everyone nervously shifted in their seats as the president moved hesitantly around the side of the large conference table, thinking as he walked. He slowly continued advancing simultaneously toward myself and the general, who was now standing in much too close proximity to me. Once the president reached our position, he stopped and took a moment to address the others in the situation room. "Does anyone else have anything to add?"

"Just that the robot is now in Moscow and has just vaporized the Ministry of Defense building," said the CIA Director in a strained and dejected tone of voice, while looking back in curiosity at the president. No one else in the situation room offered any comments.

"Thank you. Anyone else?" asked the president as he exchanged glances with everyone in the situation room. The question was greeted with a moody silence throughout the room. I could sense nerves were stretching tight among this group of elite individuals.

A noticeable gloomy, heart-sinking despair produced a faintly unnatural atmosphere throughout the situation room. It was readily apparent to me that everyone was looking painfully uncomfortable. I could only imagine what I looked like to the others. I felt tired, a bit embarrassed, and probably looked a little disheveled as well. I had no doubt the president was struggling with all the opinions expressed in the last few minutes. This was the one time in my life that I was happy not to be the one who had to make the decision as to how we were to proceed. I breathed a small prayer for the president. I was startled as he lightly touched my arm and spoke.

"Dr. Benson, as I have said, I appreciate the insight you have shared with us today. I fully understand your point of military resistance to the robot being a futile gesture. Believe me, in light of everything we have witnessed here the past few hours, I understand that point all too well. However, as president of these united states, I believe I could not in good conscience stand by and watch helplessly, and do nothing as our country is decimated. If, as you have said, our governments have gotten us into this situation, then it would be incumbent of this government to do everything in its considerable power to try and get us out of the mess we have caused. I, therefore, feel compelled to take some type of military action against this invader. Make no mistake, Dr. Benson, I must try."

The president turned his attention to the general in command of the Joint Chiefs of Staff.

"General," said the president as he put his hand on the shoulder of the general, "I want some military options on my desk within the next two hours. We don't have much time, so please act with all due speed."

"In the meantime," the president continued as he turned back toward me, "Dr. Benson, I want you to work unceasingly with my staff to come up with some options on how to approach this robot with the expressed intent of establishing some rudiment form of communication with it. I will order all available assistance to be placed at your disposal. If there is anything you need, just let the vice president know of your requirements."

The president then turned and faced the entire assembly, and spoke to no one in particular. "I will return in two hours . . . that would be approximately . . . 0330 hours. I sincerely hope each of you will expend your best efforts to obtain some workable solutions to this threat."

"Thank you, Mr. President," everyone responded simultaneously. We all watched with great interest as the president turned and strode briskly out of the room. The general of the Joint Chiefs of Staff offered a quick, scornful stare in my direction then turned and followed the president out of the same door. As it closed behind him, I looked at the rest of the assembled personnel in the room. All eyes were looking at me in an appraising and expectant manner. I felt my heart jump.

"This is just great," I thought to myself as I slowly moved back toward the conference table. "How the hell do I get myself into these situations?"

"Well, everyone," I cleared my voice and announced in the most authoritative manner I could summon, "we have a lot to do and a short time to do it in. So it goes without saying I am going to need everyone's help and cooperation to the fullest extent. If anyone wants to take a moment to say a short prayer, please do so now. We may not have the luxury of time to do so later."

Chapter Seven

Events Escalate

0330
22 Dec 2012
Washington, D.C.

There was a significant, mounting excitement and surprise when the president unexpectedly reentered the stale atmosphere of the situation room at exactly 0330 hours. No one had bothered to look at their watch or any of the clocks on the walls in an effort to keep track of time. The truth was we were simply too much engrossed into our missions. As I looked around the faces at the table, one could readily observe how tired we all were. The president, on the other hand, looked quite a bit more refreshed than we did, having allowed himself a fresh shave, shower, and a clean set of clothes.

The president's unanticipated entrance had elicited a nervous restlessness throughout the situation room. I absolutely had no doubt many in the room may have felt a similar sense of anxiety I was feeling. I am quite sure many sensed a mixture of anxiety and misery. As a direct contrast, the president's demeanor appeared sharply more energetic. It was plainly evident he was looking more relaxed than when he had left the room roughly two hours ago. He strode immediately to his seat and signaled with a curt, slight gesture for the assembled to sit as well. Once everyone had become seated at the table, the president abruptly turned to his vice president and spoke. His voice, once again, a resonant force behind the quietly spoken words.

"Mr. Vice President, let's begin with you. Could you please give me an update on the activities of the robot?"

"Yes, of course, Mr. President," began the vice president as he squirmed restlessly in his seat, while shuffling the papers in his hand. "The robot has devastated all of Russia. The city of Moscow has ceased to exist. A partial list of areas and facilities attacked besides all those in Moscow are as follows:

The All-Russian Scientific Research Institute for Experimental Physics located in Sarov

The All-Russian Scientific Research Institute for Technical Physics in Snezhinsk

The All-Russian Institute of Automatics in Moscow

The Research Institute of Measuring Systems in Nizhniy Novgorod

The Russian Ministry of Defense Fourth Central Scientific Research Institute of Strategic Rocket Forces, located in—"

"Thank you. I get the picture," interrupted the president as he guided his vice president to a different type of discussion. "Have we heard anything from prime minister or president of the Soviet Union?"

"No, Mr. President. All communication links between the USA and the Soviet Republic have been terminated. We were able to gather some early preliminary casualty figures, which came in before our communication with the Russians had been terminated. All of the preliminary intelligence reports we have obtained indicated figures of an attack fatality rate slightly over 100 million. Mr. President, the last known population figure of the Soviet Republic was in the neighborhood of 145 million! The casualty count of the wounded was slightly over 25. We can successfully extrapolate from those figures that when the robot attacks an area, complete annihilation can be expected. The robot does not wound, it kills. The few wounds suffered by the unfortunate individuals who survived the attack were said to be similar to radiation burns. In time, those wounds may well turn out to be lethal. However, at this time, we just don't have any specific way of knowing.

"Every single one of our intelligence sources on the ground inside Russia have been effectively silenced. We have had no visual reference from inside Russia for the last hour or so. All nuclear-related facilities, including nuclear submarine pens, and all air force bases designated as nuclear air bases have been destroyed. We also have had reports that all nuclear submarines of any and all nationalities . . . have been destroyed. Mr. President, any nuclear-powered vessel representing any nation, anywhere, has been destroyed. These occurrences had apparently taken place when the spaceship flew over the affected areas, but the communist veil of secrecy prevented any leak of information about those events at the real time they occurred."

"That's just like the Russians," muttered the secretary of Defense. The vice president ignored the comment and continued on with his report.

"Somehow, the spaceship was able to detect these submarines at depths of over 1500 feet. The Soviet Shark class submarine, the Typhoon, and the Borey Class submarines, the Yury Dolgoruky, the Alexander Nevsky, and the Vladimir Monomakh have been out of radio communication since the spacecraft passed over the area. The Soviets have acknowledged our assumption that those nuclear class submarines were lost with all hands aboard. Mr. President, all knowledgeable sources lead us to conclude there truly seems to be no safe place to hide from the robot. Not on the Earth, below the Earth, or in its seas. There just is no ultimate safe place. This intruder is not playing any favorites. All nations, whether they have nuclear capabilities or not, are at risk."

"I am afraid I must fully agree with your assessment," replied the president as he pulled at his chin in a very agitated manner. "I do not hesitate to confess my loss of confidence in our military's ability to do anything to stop what is about to happen to our country."

"Also, Mr. President," the voice of the FBI Director jumped into the conversation in his usual calm manner, "our latest intelligence reports indicate the robot has begun an attack against Israel within the past hour. Although our Israeli friends have always maintained the strictest, the most secret, policy about their nuclear capabilities, it was widely thought they possessed a very sizeable nuclear arsenal. However, since their nuclear program was established in the 1950s, we have been unable to uncover any facts or findings allowing us a true picture of the size of their nuclear arsenal. Since the FBI has been coordinating their efforts with the CIA—"

"Where is the director of the CIA, and for that matter, the NSC chief?" asked the president as he interrupted with a noticeable bit of annoyance in his voice.

"Both the director of the CIA and the NSC chief will be here directly, Mr. President," interjected the White House chief of staff as he was just finishing an important conversation on his cell phone. "It seems panic and chaos is beginning to increase in the streets . . . making travel more difficult. Both NSC chief and the director of the CIA are entering the underground parking facility as we speak."

"Thanks, Scott, I appreciate it," responded the president as he slipped back into the comfortable regions of his chair and resumed his intense stare at the FBI director. "Please, continue with what you were saying. I apologize for my interruption."

"Yes, thank you, Mr. President." As the FBI director began again with his briefing, he had wearily stood up and moved next to a large map of the East and was now pointing directly at the country of Israel.

"We know the Israeli's nuclear program is centered at the Negev Nuclear Research Center here, just outside of the town of Dimona. We can theorize that based upon the capabilities of the Dimona reactor, the Israelis used to have an arsenal of about two hundred nuclear devices. I say "used to have," Mr. President, because the robot chose Dimona as his primary target of choice since entering Israel. Their plutonium extraction plant, uranium purification plant, as well as the uranium conversion and fuel fabrication facilities have all been vaporized . . . utterly destroyed. The spaceship and robot have since implemented a sweeping swath of destruction heading due north, destroying the town of Beersheeba, parts of Jerusalem, and Moshav Zekharya, here. The nuclear weapons storage facility at Tirosh has also been devastated as well as the air base located nearby to the nuclear gravity bomb storage bunkers at Tel Nof. Apparently, the final targets in Israel designated for destruction by the robot were the nuclear weapons assembly facility at Yodefat in northern Israel, and the nuclear weapons storage facility at Eilabun, here, Mr. President."

"I see," replied the president succinctly. "Where is the spaceship now?"

"The spacecraft has just recently departed the country of Israel. Of the 7 million plus population of Israel, early reports indicate, compared to previous countries attacked by the robot, fatalities were actually rather light. Initial reports coming in haphazardly indicate a number of only one million killed, ten wounded. Shared intelligence reports indicate no damage was inflicted upon the capital of Tel Aviv. Perhaps, Mr. President, the Jews are still God's chosen people," snorted the FBI director, as he threw down the reports he had been quoting.

"They always have been," I replied laconically.

"OK, the spaceship left Israel. Where is it now?" asked the president, pressing for the current location while obviously ignoring my last remark.

"Getting intelligence on the spacecraft is getting more difficult with each country destroyed, Mr. President. However, preliminary reports suggest the spacecraft is close to entering Germany."

"How many countries in the projected flight path of the spaceship have nuclear capabilities?" asked the president as he arose from his chair, advancing slowly toward the map. His face was wrinkled in thought.

"That, Mr. President, is impossible to even speculate upon. Most of those countries were satellites of the old Soviet Socialist Republic. Since they have broken away from Russia, we really don't have much of a clue as to where many of those nuclear weapons are currently located. Just a moment, Mr. President," said the FBI director as he was handed a sheet of paper from a staff personnel who had just entered the room. "I am sorry to report, Mr. President, that the Incirlik Air Base, just east of Adana, Turkey, has also just been confirmed as being a target. Reports indicate 100 percent fatalities. Mr. President, the air base contained a USAF staff of roughly five thousand airmen. The report from the Turkey Atomic Energy Agency (TAEK) goes on to state the nuclear power plant scheduled to come on line in 2014 at the Black Sea port of Sinop has also come under attack and destroyed. The spaceship seems to be cutting a wider swath of destruction than we had originally estimated. It seems to be approximately two hundred miles in width as it flies over the countries of Bulgaria and Rumania. We can only speculate the intelligence directing the spaceship and the robot must have detected some nuclear capabilities in those countries as well. It seems our enemy is very well briefed on the location of all the world's nuclear facilities and nuclear weapons."

It was at this point that both the director of the CIA and the National Security Council chief came through one of the doors of the situation room. They walked together with a strident purpose to their respective chairs and sat down without a word. They looked as tired and disgusted as the rest of the personnel assembled in the room.

"Welcome back," stated the president in a flat, monotone voice. "I hope you have some encouraging information and analysis to share with us."

It was the director of the CIA who hesitantly responded to the president's prompt. He rubbed his ear and looked dissatisfied. He cleared his throat then spoke.

"In truth, Mr. President, we have had some, shall we say, partial success in our ability to translate a portion or a measure of the alien language presented to us by Dr. Benson. However, because there was no known human reference to base analysis upon, our computers could only rely upon a common basis of known language. This fact made the task immensely more difficult. We still have a full complement of personnel working on decoding the language, but I must warn everyone progress is going to be painfully slow, I am afraid."

"Understood," stated the president, looking somewhat uncomfortable again. It seemed at that moment the president became somewhat resigned to the fate apparently in store for the future of this nation. The alien force we were facing seemed to be unstoppable and irresistible. The phrase from the old series of *Star trek the Next Generation* came suddenly into my mind: "Resistance is futile."

"Mr. President," the voice was that of Homeland Security chief, "I apologize for the interruption, but I thought you would like to know that widespread rioting has begun in some of our major cities, including right here in Washington, D.C."

"That's just great," snorted the president.

"New York, Los Angeles, San Francisco, and Chicago are also reporting small-scale rioting and chaos as well. Mr. President, I believe declaring martial law is in order. We must act now to stop the rioting and the looting. Crowd control has now become an imperative. I believe we must act immediately to prevent widespread destruction within in our cities."

"I agree with the Homeland Security chief," chimed in the voice of the FBI director. "The FBI can work together with Homeland Security in rooting out these terrorists and putting an end to the disruption."

"Mr. President, may I be permitted to speak?" I asked in an insistently polite manner.

"Of course, Dr. Benson," said the president as he reached for a cup of coffee that had just been placed next to him on the table by a staffer, "I value all opinions."

"I am afraid you won't like it, but here goes anyway. You all have sworn an oath to uphold, defend, and protect the Constitution of the United States against all enemies, foreign and domestic. Yet each one of you in office has consistently spit on and defiled the Constitution of the United States of America! You have rejected the very sacred oath you have sworn to uphold. This has been done by disregarding the second amendment in having the right of citizens to bear arms to protect themselves and their families, the fourth amendment against the unreasonable searches and seizures, the tenth amendment stating the powers not delegated to the United States by the constitution shall be reserved to each of the respective states, and the—"

"Mr. President, we don't have time for this type of nonsense—" the enraged voice of the director of Homeland Security said cuttingly. The director was stopped by the president who raised his hand and nodded his assent as a signal to halt the impending bickering.

"Dr. Benson, in the interest of brevity, as my Homeland Security director so eloquently stated, time is of the essence. If you have a point you wish to make, please do so at this time."

"Very well, Mr. President. My point is this. The people of the United States should not have any more of their freedom curtailed than this government has already done. These people are scared. They need to have the freedom to move away from the impending devastation of their homes. They need to save themselves and their families. These people do not need the military to treat them as terrorists. The military should be there to assist them in their efforts to save themselves. What these people need is to have their president come on national television, before we lose that capability altogether, and to give them an honest assessment of the situation . . . to calm their fears with reason. Do you want what may be your last official act as president to be declaring martial law, effectively destroying the Constitution of the United States, which is something every other president of the United States has been able to avoid? Even in time of war?"

The president seemed to pause for a few moments to take my argument into consideration. All eyes were riveted on the president. He leaned forward upon his elbows, which were setting squarely on the conference table.

As we all nervously awaited the president's response, it suddenly occurred to me that the deeper and darker theme of calling for martial law was the complete takeover of the United States by its own government, the government that was supposed to be "by the people, of the people, for the people." The government of the United States, whether Republican or Democrat, had for a hundred years or more, been stealing certain inalienable rights away from the people. Some of the purloining was accomplished by stealthy means, at other times by out-and-out power grabs. The true shame lies with the American people. Not once had they done anything to resist the continual efforts of government to seize those constitutional rights bequeathed to us by our founding fathers. It seemed to me as long as most Americans were fat and happy at home watching their sacred television and drinking beer, they couldn't care less about the freedoms they had just surrendered. Now, with the declaration of a "national emergency," and the resultant "martial law," those in power in the government would have the perfect excuse to shred the constitution completely. This act would complete the full takeover of the United States by government forces. Under the present circumstances, however, it would be short-lived. Of that I was sure. Perhaps, after all, the American people deserved this fate.

"Dr. Benson," began the president as he stared directly at me, "your point is well taken. However, if the people are to survive the upcoming holocaust that is apparently being forced upon us by this malevolent, extraterrestrial force, then it is my sincere belief this country is going to need the military in charge to prevent widespread chaos. With a strong military presence to help facilitate the evacuation of any area of our country targeted by the robot, many lives may be saved."

The president swiveled suddenly in his chair, turning toward the secretary of Homeland Security. He made very little effort to carefully conceal his mounting excitement. His next few words quivered in my brain.

"Please have the order for martial law prepared for my immediate signature. We shall initiate this at 0700 this morning."

"Yes, Mr. President."

The Homeland Security director was promptly excused from the table. As the director of Homeland Security turned quickly and walked away from the table to a far corner of the situation room, I swallowed uneasily as I observed a telephone call I and many Americans had so long feared.

"Let us, once again, proceed with the briefing, shall we?" said the president with a gesture of impatience. He now turned his attention to the director of the CIA. "Mr. Director, what have you been able to translate from Dr. Benson's notes?"

"Well, Mr. President," began the director as he had risen to his feet and began distributing some paperwork to the president, myself, and the rest of the assemblage. "I must first of all establish that what small amount we have deciphered, is within an 89.6 percent probability of accuracy, according to our computers. In Klaatu's purported communication to his home planets, which transpired from within the spacecraft, the computers have been able to come up with a partially translated transcript. The words *Imray Klaatu Narawak* can be loosely translated as *This is Klaatu reporting*. The words *Monkro Bavall baratu* roughly translate to *have made contact with*. We believe the next word *Londesko* either represents the word *Earth* or more probable, *designated planet or target*. The words *yobo teri axal* translate roughly into *governments, people, or beings, are uncooperative*. The words *balenko, buringy, and dinkus*, remain indecipherable at this time. So the first part of the message we were able to translate reads as follows: 'This is Klaatu reporting . . . have made contact with the people or governments of Earth or designated planet . . . and they are largely uncooperative at this time.' This is followed by the indecipherable content, which we are still working on as we speak."

"And the second part of the message, the one where Dr. Benson states his mother is inside the ship with Klaatu prior to the spaceman addressing the assembled crowd of scientists and leaders?" asked the president stirring nervously in his chair. Both men seemed to gaze suspiciously at each other for a moment.

"Yes, that one is a bit more difficult to translate, Mr. President, but we have had some small success with this portion of the transcript as well," stated the director of the CIA in a modest and reserved manner. "The first three words Klaatu spoke were *Declaro Dorexi ubo*, which translates roughly to *I am in final stages of preparation to depart*. This is followed by the words *Bosfor, Nowaki, Bixlo*, which remain indecipherable at this time. We were, however, able to translate the next two words *Atlango and Candall* as meaning *recommend observing situation*. The following words *Loto, Marata, Eckla, and Boros* remain indecipherable to us at this time. The words *Quistolo and Pasloxo* translate either into *imminent destruction, or future destruction*. Our computers could not differentiate between the two and has proffered probabilities of accuracy for both translations at 82.6 percent. The words following those, *Pilaro and Corteka* are indecipherable at this time. Finally, the last two words recorded by Mrs. Benson were those of *Raymi and Okro*, which our computers have translated as *final message before departure*. So roughly translated, the message in parts reads, 'I am in the final stages of preparing to depart from this planet,' then indecipherable, then ' . . . I recommend observing this planet . . . ' followed by indecipherable, followed by ' . . . their imminent destruction and/or future destruction,' followed by words which are as of yet, indecipherable.

"The final words of Klaatu's closing message were ' . . . this is my final message before departing.' That is what we have been able to decipher to this point, Mr. President. As I have stated, we are continuing to work on the words we have as yet been unable to decode. Computer analysis states there is a 92.7 percent probability the entire message may be deciphered in an estimated time frame of thirty-four hours."

"I don't think we have thirty-four hours, Mr. Director. But for what you have been able to decipher at this time . . . thank you, and well done," said the president with a small nod of his head and a smile of gratitude. His voice seem to grow quieter as he turned his attention toward me. As his eyes widened suspiciously, and with a look of expectation, the president asked the question I knew was coming and dreaded to hear. "Dr. Benson, has anyone come up with a plausible method of establishing some form of contact or communication with the robot?"

"Since all satellite and radio communication with the robot and the spaceship is impossible due to the electrical dampening effect and other significant interference we have encountered, and since we also do not have any idea of the effective radius of the dampening area, I'm am afraid any communication is necessarily going to have to occur in a . . . face-to-face method. We had thought of using a bullhorn to try and establish communication, but I have a fear the sound coming out of the bullhorn will be too distorted to be effective. We simply cannot afford any mistakes in this attempt. Someone is literally going to have to place themselves within yards, or even feet, of the robot in an attempt to establish communications. If, for any reason, Gort does not acknowledge either the method or the message of the communication, then the unfortunate messenger will most assuredly perish in the effort."

"I see," said the president as he let a long, slow gasp of horrified understanding escape through his pursed lips. The president's eyes assumed a deep and hollow look. After a small, but intense, period of silence, the president turned to the CIA director and spoke decisively, "As Dr. Benson states, there is apparently no other option. What must be, must be. I need an operative that would volunteer for what could very possibly turn out to be a suicide mission. This mission is going to take someone with nerves of steel, and someone that—"

"Excuse me, Mr. President," I interrupted forcefully, and with an oddly cold formality, "Asking for a volunteer will not be necessary. It is essential that I be the one to do this."

"Dr. Benson, I appreciate your patriotism . . ."

"It is not patriotism, Mr. President. It is pure logic. Even our computers agree, I am the logical one. I am the only one who has seen Gort up close. I am, also, the only one who has personal knowledge concerning the robot. Quite frankly, Mr. President, I am the only expert on the robot or the spaceship you have nearby and available. Logic, therefore, dictates this responsibility should necessarily fall on me."

"Dr. Benson," the voice was that of the White House chief of staff. "I remember you once confided to me these aliens created a . . . race . . . of robots. Chances are this may not even be the same one that visited this planet in 1951."

"It may not be, Scott, but if my theory on this race of robots is correct, then each robot is encoded with the same pertinent data as the next. Each robot possesses in their memory banks the identical information that the other possesses. Therefore, each robot possesses in its accumulated data processes . . . my image and my voice pattern."

"Excuse me, Doctor, but you spoke to the robot?" asked the president in a puzzled tone of voice. He had risen uneasily from his seat. I stood up as well, waiting patiently, and watched as the president moved around the table. As he slowly approached me, I could see him staring at me with appraising eyes.

"I did, Mr. President, and though I was only nine years old at the time, there is a chance my image, although altered by age, and my voice pattern data, could very well be encoded into Gort's memory. If it is, whether it is the exact same robot or a duplicate, it should retain the ability to acknowledge and recognize the sound of my voice. The robot should, theoretically, acknowledge my image as well. Also, since I befriended Klaatu, it seems likely the robot may have observed the result of that friendship, or perhaps, even more likely, Klaatu may have encoded that friendship into the robot's memory. If any of those events hold true, then there is a distinct possibility, if I could somehow position myself near enough to the robot to establish a communication link, I could successfully establish communication with Gort. Either way, like it or not, Mr. President, I am the best hope you have at stopping the robot."

"Mr. President," the CIA director interrupted in a calm, but high voice, "the robot has now started attacking Germany. Initial reports indicate the nuclear reactor sites at Isar and Niederaichbach have been destroyed, along with the nuclear reactor site located in Temelin, in the Czech Republic. These intelligence reports indicate that the city of Munich has been at least partially destroyed. Switzerland is in the process of evacuating all of their nuclear reactor sites along their northern border as a precautionary measure. Attack reports are also slowly coming in from the countries of Greece, Italy, Bulgaria, Romania, Hungary, the Ukraine . . ."

"What does the current computer time estimate indicate . . . before the robot is done with its mission in Europe, and heads across the ocean to the United States?" asked the president as he slowly walked back to his seat and slumped dejectedly down into its soft confines.

"All computer estimates indicate . . . at this current rate of destruction, the spaceship will be approaching our East Coast within two and a half to three hours. Since I don't see anything deterring it, I would have to agree with those estimates. We, of course, have no idea where the robot will land upon U.S. soil. It is anyone's guess as to where it will commence its destructive efforts. Mr. President, I strongly suggest we initiate a class 1 evacuation of the White House. It is also my recommendation that at this time the president evacuate to the secondary command site outside the area of Washington, D.C."

"Very well," replied the president, dejectedly.

"I also suggest the vice president should be relocated out of Washington to the Omaha site. This should also be an immediate evacuation. If we wait until the spaceship is approaching the United States, we may not have the ability of movement. As evidenced by past events, once this country comes under the umbrella of the electrical interference generated by the ship . . ."

"Yes, I see your point. Let's evacuate and disperse in accordance with operational plan delta. Would you please see to the arrangements. My family and I will leave the White House in thirty minutes," responded the president as he began to pick up assorted paperwork.

"Dr. Benson, where do you intend to intercept the robot?"

"Mr. President, I believe it would be clearly impossible for me to get close enough to the robot in any big city environment. Trying to contact Gort in New York City, Washington, D.C., . . . or any large metropolis would prove to be fruitless and fatal in my opinion. I could not get close enough to Gort through the rubble and mass of panicked and hysterical people that would most likely accompany the targeted area."

"So, Dr. Benson, you are seriously considering abandoning the whole East Coast of the United States?" asked the president in an incredulous manner, his eyes a look of blank bewilderment.

"I do not see that there are many options, Mr. President. We have got to try and plot an intercept course somewhere in the mid-west, perhaps at the Paducah Gaseous Diffusion Plant in Kentucky. Hell. Mr. President, I may have to go as far west as the Los Alamos National laboratory in New Mexico, or Minot Air Force Base in North Dakota. Perhaps the location of Nellis Air Force Base in Nevada should be seriously considered, as this would more than likely be a primary target for Gort. Nellis is one of the air forces' two main nuclear weapons depots. The problem is, Mr. President, I am going to have to either approach Gort on foot, or just pop up suddenly from some type of hiding spot. Anyway, this means I need a place where it is open enough to meet Gort one-on-one. I have to position myself far enough out from the intended target site to approach Gort before he begins his assault. However, I cannot be so far out that he passes my location, or lands his ship closer to the intended target area. I won't get a second chance on this, Mr. President. I have to be as precise as I can possibly be. I must get it right the first time."

"Mr. President," interjected the director of the CIA as he appeared to be reading more reports, "we now have discernable evidence the nuclear power plants at Fessenheim, Germany, Beznau, just north of Zurich in Switzerland, and also Goesgen, and Muehlberg, just outside of Bern, Switzerland, and the Lucens nuclear power plants have all been attacked and destroyed. The surrounding cities and countrysides have been decimated. These reports state pretty much the same as all our previous intelligence on these attacks have stated . . . many have been killed, not many wounded. There is now a very large problem with refugees amassing in unaffected areas. This latest intelligence summary is indicating the robot has turned due north and has just initiated attacks against the Grundremmingen nuclear power plant outside of Ulm, Germany. Also the commanding officers of Ramstein Air Force Base and Spangdahlem Air Force Base are requesting orders to either engage the threat or evacuate the area. Our air force bases in Stuttgart, which is in close proximity to where the robot is currently attacking at Gundremmingen, have discontinued communication. We must suppose our air bases in Germany are either currently under attack or soon will be."

"My God," uttered the president as he froze in his tracks, "what other bases do we have in the vicinity?"

"We have the air force base in Heidleberg, which contain the Patton Barracks, the Air Force Base Coleman at Mannheim-Sandhofen, the Katterbach Barracks located at Ansbach, and the Air Station Einsiedlerhof at Kaiserslautern. Actually, Mr. President, we have quite a few other bases in Germany as well. I can get a complete list of all U.S. bases located in Germany in about ten minutes."

"Never mind that. For immediate execution . . . inform all commanding officers at all bases in Germany in particular and Europe in general to evacuate personnel into the surrounding countrysides. Have them find and take shelter to the best of their ability. And may God help them because we sure as hell can't!" fumed the president as he kicked his chair out of the way in disgust.

The president wheeled about suddenly.

"Inform the French and British authorities of our decision and suggest to them they follow the same routine. They should know by now that none of our world's technology is going to halt this robot. If they haven't guessed it by now, let them know that the American cavalry will not be riding to their rescue. Hell, when the time comes, we won't even be able to help ourselves," snapped the president in disgust.

"Yes, Mr. President. I will ensure the communication goes out immediately," replied the CIA director, quickly picking up one of the numerous phones in the room. I watched with interest as the director pressed two numbers, turned away from the rest of us, and began speaking. The president, once again, turned his attention back to me. Reaching into his suit's left front inner pocket and producing a cell phone, he began to walk toward me as he spoke.

"Dr. Benson, I want to give you this cell phone. It only has one number on it, so just open it up and press send. This will ring straight into my cell, which I will have on my person at all times. I want you to maintain contact with me at all costs. Leave immediately for your best destination to confront Gort. Once you are ready, please call me. Do not wait too long, for once the spaceship arrives on the continental United States, my guess is that all telephonic communications will be terminated as we come under the spaceship's umbrella of interference. You may require anything from this office, and it will be yours.

Just let my chief of staff know what you want, and he will have the authority to produce it."

The president held up his arm and looked at his watch. His eyes locked on to mine.

"It's approximately 0419 hours. I already have a Raptor waiting for you at Andrews Air Force Base to fly you to whatever site you choose to intercept the robot. I consider it absolutely essential to the survival of our country that you are successful in your endeavor. Take all measures you deem necessary. We all are counting on you. The whole country is counting on you. Well, Dr. Benson, I guess that pretty much covers it . . . other than to say good luck and Godspeed."

"Thank you, Mr. President," I said as I shook his hand in a fairly anxious manner. His handshake seemed to have a steadying effect on me.

"I wish you and your family the very best of luck, and I hope you and your family will be safe. Good luck to you, sir, and may God help us all."

As I turned and headed toward the exit accompanied by the White House chief of staff, I could not help but feel a twinge of sadness as the thought hit my mind that, one way or the other, this would probably be the last time I see the president or any of his staff alive. As we approached the door, I turned slightly and surveyed the situation room for one last time, reflecting upon the events of the night. After we closed the door behind us, I turned to Scott.

"Scotty, if at all possible, get you and your family as far away from the president and his staff as you can. Find yourself a nice little deserted area to take refuge in, and hunker down until all this is over," I implored him as we walked.

"I am afraid my place is at the side of the president," replied Scott as we entered an outer room where I could see through several large glass doors in front of us. Through the doors I could see outside to a grassy area where a helicopter was just beginning to turn its rotors. "Now tell me what you need and I will ensure you get it."

"How about the ravioli?"

Chapter Eight

And So It Begins . . .

0445
22 Dec 2012
Andrews Air Force Base

As I climbed out of the VH-3/VH-60 Marine Two Helicopter, whose regular duty is to fly the vice president to various destinations, I could not help but be impressed by the proficiency of the flight crew. I was informed during the short flight from the White House lawn to Andrews Air Force Base that there are always more than eight hundred Marines supervising the complete operation of Marine One and Marine Two. This unit is based out of Quantico, Virginia, under the name of Marine Helicopter Squadron One (HMX-1) and are called "the Night Hawks."

I had expected to see a couple of Marines in flight suits, so I was pleasantly surprised to see the pilot and copilot, as well as the rest of the flight crew, dressed in the Marine Blue Dress/Charlie uniform. I was also very much surprised to find out that when flying the president to some location, there was always up to five identical helicopters flying in formation. This was in a coordinated effort to confuse any would be presidential assassins. These spit and polished young men and women were always willing to put their life on the line while flying the president or vice president. Marine One and Two, along with the look-alike decoy helicopters, are equipped with standard military antimissile defense technologies and countermeasures to counter any threat in the air or on the ground. President Eisenhower was the commander in chief who initiated the proceedings to establish the mission of HMX-1. This mission was originally assigned to the Army and the Marines until 1976, when the Marines were given exclusivity over carrying out the mission of providing secure helicopter transport to the president and vice president.

It wasn't long before this mission was soon expanded to flying the secretary of Defense, the secretary of the navy, the commandant of the Marine Corps, and all visiting heads of state, as well as flying various VIPs to important destinations. Considering this to be the case, apparently I had become a very important person. The White House military office had seen to everything concerned with my short flight to Andrews, and although I am not particularly fond of flying, the treatment extended to me by the flight crew was exemplary. I personally thanked each of them before I disembarked from the aircraft. Men and women of the highest order . . . all of them!

As I turned away from the helicopter, I was immediately struck by a very satisfying and reassuring sight. There on the flight tarmac roughly fifty yards directly in front of me was a very familiar F-22 Raptor. I could feel myself smiling broadly as I recognized the figure of Major Jack Holloway executing his usual preflight check of the aircraft. I broke into a small jog to cover the distance to the aircraft, extending my hand to the major as I neared his location. His rugged face broke into a strange smile as he reached out to shake my hand.

"Major Jack Holloway, you're a damn good sight for my old and sore eyes to rest upon! How the hell are you?" I asked as I broke out into a small genuine laugh. Major Holloway merely shrugged his shoulders indifferently, winked, and responded.

"Can't complain, Doc. Hell, it wouldn't do no good if I did," he said in a booming voice, with a now expansive, enveloping smile. Jack Holloway's manner and apparent enthusiasm had a very immediate calming effect upon me. There is no one else I would rather have flying me to my destination. I felt very comfortable in his capable hands, fond of flying or not. I instantly decided to enlist his help in identifying the best location to intercept Gort.

"Jack," I said as I grabbed his arm and pulled him closer to me, "I am in need of your help."

"I have been briefed and ordered to give you whatever assistance I can render, up to the highest security classification. Nothing is off-limits. So run your idea up the flagpole, and we'll see who salutes it, Doc. What have you got?"

"I am making a guess you have flown into a lot of air bases here in the U.S., haven't you?"

"I probably have hit most of them, why?"

"I've been tasked with the mission of intercepting the spaceship and robot at some location which would prove a likely target for a future assault. I need a somewhat isolated air base that produces some sort of cover out at its perimeter. I need some form of basic concealment to allow me the ability to get within speaking distance of the robot. I assure you, I have no desire to be instantly disintegrated by the robot, so a well-concealed location out away from the crowded interior of the air base is essential to the success of this operation. And whatever concealment exists cannot have any military application, otherwise it will draw the fire of the robot. The air base we choose must necessarily have some type of nuclear weapons stored within its confines, or at least be near a nuclear facility of some type, as the apparent mission of the robot is to eliminate all nuclear capabilities of every country in the world."

"I see," said Major Holloway as he scratched his chin in thought.

"Also, Jack, and this goes without needing to be said, but I'll say it anyway, time is of the essence. The location chosen needs to be a base we can get to within two hours or less. It has been estimated the robot will reach our eastern shores somewhere around 0700 to 0730. That is when the attack on the United States will commence. Once the attack begins, I believe there will be no reasonable capability of either flight or communication. So I'm going to be pretty much on my own once this event begins. Jack, what air base would you recommend that would best suit my purpose?"

"Hell, Doc, there's a whole list of potential candidates I can think of: Barskdale Air Force Base, Louisiana, has gravity bombs, air-launched cruise missiles, advanced cruise missiles, and is the main base for our B-52H bombers. Then there's Whiteman Air Force Base in Missouri. They have various gravity bombs designated for the B-2 bombers there. Minot Air Force base in North Dakota houses around 150 minuteman III intercontinental missiles and a wing of B-52H bombers, but I don't think we could reach that in time. It would be close. The same with Malmstrom Air Force Base in Montana. Warren Air Force Base in Wyoming took a pretty good hit when the Cheyenne Mountain Complex next to it was destroyed. And this isn't even mentioning the 450 to 500 ICBM sites scattered throughout the rocky mountain states and the Dakotas. But if you were to ask me the number one site I would pick . . . Nellis Air Force Base. Yes, Doc, Nevada would be my logical choice."

"Sounds good, so far, Jack"

"Nellis is one of two main nuclear storage depots in the United States. Besides storing nuclear tipped weapons at this facility, gravity bombs and air-launched cruise missiles are also stored at Nellis. As to flight time, once airborne, if I punch it, I think we can make it just in time. It will require afterburners all the way, and a midflight refueling, Doc. You up to it?"

"Nellis Air Force Base it is, Jack. Thanks. Now let's suit up and hit the road . . . er . . . I mean, sky."

The F-22 Raptor's Pratt and Whitney's engines roared to life, and soon, Major Jack Holloway had the aircraft turned into the long runway authorized for our immediate use. With an even greater roar than our previous flight, and a sizeable jolt, Jack, good to his word, "punched it" and we began to speed down the runway at a rapidly increasing velocity. In a moment, we were airborne and rapidly angling our way to a higher altitude. The force of the gravity slammed me back into my seat, continually pressing steadily against me as we climbed. The feeling was quite dreadful, but exhilarating. As I turned my head to look out the F-22's canopy toward the ground, I could see the earth slipping away with excessive rapidity. It was a beautiful sight to behold. It did not seem to take the aircraft but a minute or two to reach forty thousand feet. As we leveled out, Major Holloway came on the ship's intercom.

"You all right back there, Dr. Benson?"

"Roger that, Jack." I replied in a shaky voice, trying to regain what little composure I had left. Once we had climbed above the partial cloud layer, the view was even more magnificent. Clear blue skies all around, with just a few wisps of fluffy, white clouds below. I found myself absentmindedly observing the terrain moving by below us and was lost momentarily in my thoughts. I was only slightly startled when the voice of Major Holloway came across the intercom embedded in my flight helmet.

"Hey, Doc, I'm receiving a transmission from Air Force One. Patching it through now."

"Dr. Benson, can you hear me?" the voice was the president of the United States.

"Yes, sir, loud and clear, over," I replied.

"Thought it important for you to know that the robot has finished laying waste to both Germany and France and is currently attacking Great Britain. England is being turned into burned-out ruins as we speak. Subsequently, all communication with them and the European continent has ceased. England has only a few nuclear-related facilities: the Faslane Naval Base where the Vanguard-class clear submarines with Trident II D-5 ballistic missiles are housed; the Atomic Weapons Establishment at Aldermaston, AWE Burghfield; the royal Naval Armament Depot at Coulport; along with Nuclear reactors outside of London and Glasgow. The Central Intelligence Agency computers now calculate that at this rate of destruction, the spaceship could be headed to the United States within a minimum of thirty-five minutes to a maximum of one hour. My family and I are headed to a safe location, if there is such a thing. What is your destination?"

"Mr. President, I am headed toward Nellis Air Force Base in Nevada. I will attempt an intercept of the robot at that location. For various reasons, this seems the optimal location to carry out my mission," I said as I noticed a patch of cloud drift by below our speeding aircraft.

"Are you sure you have the time to get there?" asked the president with a note of concern in his voice. Before I could answer, Major Holloway joined in on the conversation.

"Mr. President, this is Major Holloway. I will get the good doctor to Nellis on time. We are going afterburners all the way. We may land with an empty fuel tank, but we'll make it."

"Thank you, Major Holloway, I will leave Dr. Benson in your capable hands then," responded the president in a more calm and relaxed manner. "Dr. Benson, I want to, again, personally thank you for all your help and sacrifice in this crisis. There may be nothing we can do to stop the future destruction of our country, but I thank you with all my heart for your efforts. Good luck and Godspeed."

"Thank you, Mr. President," I replied, feeling a modicum of emotion begin to well up within me. I felt the president's wishes were very sincere and found it very satisfying and heartwarming.

"And good luck to you and your family, Mr. President. I hope we all have the good fortune to meet somewhere, sometime, after this is over. Will attempt to call you when I arrive at Nellis. Good-bye, Mr. President."

The radio intercom went dead. I suddenly felt very alone in the world, as if I was racing toward a separate and irrevocable fate from the rest of the humanity. The entire past twenty-four hours or so of events were finally beginning to catch up to me. I could sense a great weight pressing heavily down upon me. I once again began to feel very weary and extremely dejected. It was no wonder I began to think about what would be left of our country after Gort had finished with his horrible mission. I could readily imagine Washington, D.C., destroyed, New York, Boston, Arlington, Pittsburgh, Cleveland, Chicago, along with all the other great cities. Every major city destroyed, and the population decimated. There might be only a million or so survivors left in the entire country when the robot finishes with us.

As for my own safety, there also existed the very distinct possibility that there would be no way of communicating with Gort . . . no way to countermand the robot's orders. I knew if I failed, I would die. Historically, no one who gets close to Gort survives. The robot has been obviously programmed to destroy men, women, and children. Anything, including animals, that had the great misfortune to cross Gort's path simply ceased to exist in mere seconds. All completely vaporized by Gort's energy beam. Whether or not I possessed the capability to communicate with the robot, in light of my past connections with it and Klaatu, was the preeminent question. Clearly, I was staking my life on the answer being . . . yes. I must confess the thought crossed my mind that I must have been crazy to volunteer to come face to face with Gort. The chances of my surviving a confrontation with Gort, in my opinion, were very small, indeed.

"Doc, you still awake back there?" asked Major Holloway through the ship's intercom.

"Yes, I am Jack. Was just doing some thinking . . ."

"No, seriously, Doc. You know I never believed all those stories about Nostradamus, the Mayan Calendar, and the date December 21, 2012. I remember reading somewhere that the Earth, the sun, the moon, and whatever else were all going to align with the center of the universe. I figured something might happen due to gravity changes. But I never imagined this. Do you think the alignment with the center of the universe was a part of all that has happened?"

"Highly possible, Jack. Maybe some type of wormhole was opened up . . . allowing this to be the best time for interstellar space travel. We sure as hell don't know everything concerning quantum mechanics. At the very least, the alignment you're talking about could make traveling through space from the center of the universe to Earth a much easier and faster flight. Bending space and time . . . for space travel has still not been accomplished in our world, but this Association of Planets group may be able to do just that. If that is the case, they can travel an amazing distance in a short amount of time. Whether this has anything to do with the Mayan calendar or Nostradamus and his predictions, well . . . your guess is as good as mine. Could just be coincidence. We may never have a satisfactory explanation for all this."

I took a moment to scan the horizon. Jack continued the conversation.

"Once we get to Nellis, how can I help?" said Jack in a clearly concerned voice. I admired his courage in the face of what could be certain death.

"Do you have a family, Jack?" I asked.

"I have a wife. Just got married a year ago. As a matter of fact, we are stationed at Nellis Air Force base. We live in base housing. Nothing fancy, mind you. Like to have you over for dinner sometime . . . meet my wife," he responded warmly. I immediately appreciated the sincerity of his invitation. I smiled briefly at the thought of a home-cooked meal in a warm and friendly atmosphere. I shook my head clear of the vision and answered in the best way I knew how.

"Jack, believe me, I would love to do just that. However, with events unfolding as they are, it is unlikely we will ever get the chance. But truthfully, there is something you can do for me when we reach Nellis. What I want you to do is once we land . . . get to your wife immediately and get the hell off this base! If I can't stop this thing, everything and everyone on this base will be destroyed. There will be nothing you or anyone can do to stop the destruction. Do not let anyone tell you differently. I want to know at least that you and your wife are safely away from Nellis Air Force base, and safe as can be under the circumstances."

"I'm not sure I can do that, Doc. I have my duties . . ."

"Jack, listen to me very carefully. By the time the robot and spaceship arrive at this location, there will no longer be any effective military force left to be loyal to at all. Every single military base or camp east of Nellis would have been destroyed. Everyone on or around those bases would have been annihilated. We will, much as China, Russia, and the other countries of the world, be relegated to third-world country status. Hell, probably even fourth- or fifth-world country status. Damn near back to the Stone Age.

"Sounds pretty desperate, Doc."

"It is, Jack. There will no longer be a United States of America, there will only be survivors of a once-great country. The survivors will have to start almost completely over. It will be a day-to-day struggle just to continue living. I would suggest you also grab all the weapons and ammunition you can carry. You will most assuredly need that as well. Food, water, clothing, all will become essential. It is going to be pretty bleak until you can get some type of community organized. This new world we are going to find ourselves in, if we are lucky to survive, is going to need all the leaders it can get."

There was a long pause of profound silence. Finally, Major Holloway spoke in a scarcely perceptible tone of voice, belying the sadness and resignation to a fate that would not be a happy or an easy one.

"Doc . . . I don't know what to say. I have been in the air force most of my adult life. I am not sure at all that I can just run away and leave my comrades to bear the brunt of an attack. That seems pretty cowardly to me."

"Jack, believe me, it would be more cowardly to die uselessly in an action that should not be fought and could never be won. This time there will be no hope of victory. Resign yourself to that fact. The technology we are facing is so overwhelmingly advanced to ours that if they had really wanted to, the aliens could have destroyed all life on our planet from the depths of space. Believe me, they didn't even need to land on our planet to destroy it. Earth could have been turned into a burned-out cinder from a thousand miles in space. Please, Jack, I am begging you not to die uselessly. We are going to need good, strong leaders, such as yourself, to implement the rebuilding that is going to be necessary on this planet. Chances are I will more than likely not survive, but I consider it imperative men like you must."

"You make a strong case, Doc. I'll think about it. Sounds like I don't have much time to get organized," responded Jack as we gained a bit of altitude to fly over a small weather disturbance below. We must have been flying for about an hour. "You know, Doc, it seems like . . . hold on! I've got an incoming message for you from Washington. Switching to full speaker system now."

"Dr. Benson! Can you hear me?" The highly agitated voice was that of the White House chief of staff.

"This is Dr. Benson, I am reading you loud and clear. You have an update for me? Over."

"The spaceship has completely destroyed Germany, France, and England less than an hour ago. The ship has now landed outside of New York City. Major devastation and destruction is taking place as we speak. I do not know how much longer I will be able to communicate with you. I am still here in Washington. Probably only a matter of minutes before the ship arrives here. All military bases in the state of New York and on the nearby East Coast have been under attack. Portsmouth Naval shipyard in Maine gone . . ."

"Scott, listen to me! You have got to get the hell out of Washington right now! There is nothing you can do at your post anymore. Try and save yourself and your family. Over."

"I am afraid it is too late . . . nothing is moving here. All the streets are clogged . . . vehicles stalled everywhere. Severe rioting and looting is occurring . . . and . . . wait a minute . . . oh my god! I can see the spaceship emerging from the cloud cover overhead . . . communications are becoming erratic . . . beginning to fail . . . don't know how long I can—"

Abruptly, all communications from the White House chief of staff ceased. A shrill sound resonated through the static of the intercom just before Major Holloway terminated the connection.

"Sorry, Doc. Communications have been severed," announced Major Holloway in a flat, expressionless tone of voice. I'm sure the major was trying his best to sound unaffected by the communication. Perhaps he was doing that to reassure himself or to help keep me in a more calm state of being. Either way, I appreciated the effort. I could not know what fate had befallen everyone in New York City and Washington, D.C. I could only hope some people could survive the carnage inflicted upon their area.

"Doc, I'm getting communication from Nellis. Apparently the U.S. Armed Forces were incapacitated immediately upon arrival from the spaceship and have been unable to amount any type of offensive operations against the invader. Not only was Portsmouth Shipyard attacked and destroyed, but also Philadelphia Naval shipyard, Sub-base New London, and the nearby naval construction yard at Groton, Connecticut . . . have also been obliterated. Our military forces were apparently vaporized where they stood. No resistance of any kind was possible."

"I know, Jack. We have nothing technologically capable of resisting the threat."

"You know, I may be dumber than a load of bricks, Doc, but what you are saying is definitely making some sense. If the military can't stop this thing, then there sure as hell isn't going to be anything I can do to stop it."

"I am afraid that is pretty much the case . . . I'm sorry, Jack," I stated dejectedly, as I thought of the loss of all our fine young men and women in uniform who went without a complaint to their deaths. All were vaporized where they stood.

"When I was in conference with the president and his staff, I explained that very fact to the chairman of the Joint Chiefs of Staff. I told the general not to mount any offense against the spaceship or Gort. I told him it would be useless, and it would just cause the death of many good military personnel under his command. However, I was overruled by the president. I guess he felt he had to try something . . . anything."

"Well, Doc, I am beginning to see the futility of any type of resistance," he replied as a noticeable sigh escaped from his lips into the intercom. "But, damn it, Doc, there has got to be something we can do!"

"That's what the president and the general said. Militarily, there is nothing that can be done. However, there is something you can do, Jack . . . get you and your family to safety. Take care of your loved ones. Maybe that is the only thing we have left to do anymore. Maybe . . . that's all we can do . . ." I said, my voice trailing off into a mere whisper. I gathered my senses together and spoke into the intercom.

"How long until we land at Nellis? I think this is going to be closer than I thought."

"Should be there in about thirty-five minutes, Dr. Benson. That is barring any unforeseen complications," replied the major as he banked the F-22 Raptor ever so slightly to the left. The wispy clouds were whirling their way beneath us, and it seemed to me we had descended a bit in the last few minutes as well. I knew Major Holloway was in contact with control towers of various fields throughout the trip. As such, I was not wanting to engage him in any lengthy discussions. However, the mere sound of his voice seem to calm and quiet me. I must admit I always felt better after discussing events with him.

It was at this moment that an abrupt and severe jolt hit our aircraft. I could feel a severe shudder running up the length of our F-22 emanating from the tail section. This was immediately followed by several rough jerking motions as I could hear the engine begin to cut out. I could see Major Holloway fighting with the controls. After several attempts, the major was able to restart the engines.

"What's happening, Jack?" I asked as the fear within me began to rise. There was a noticeable chill sweeping through my body. I gave a slight shudder then closed my eyes while awaiting his answer.

"It seems we had a momentary systems failure. The engine had died for a few moments, but I finally got it restarted. We are back to flying under full power now, Doc."

"If the engines quit permanently, do we have enough altitude to glide into Nellis?" I asked, almost shouting into the intercom, hoping our mode of descent would be a well-controlled one. I began praying.

"I'm afraid the F-22 has the glide potential of a rock, Doc. If the engines quit for good, we may have to punch out . . . eject. Just to let you know, I have also lost all radio communication with Nellis . . . and everyone else. With events happening as they are, my guess is their radar isn't working either. Which means we are going to be pretty much on our own. Don't worry, Doc, as long as these engines work, I will get us to Nellis. I doubt there is much traffic in the air since the president initiated martial law. In any case, the closer we can get to area 1 at Nellis, the better it will be. My advice, Doc, is sit back and relax. I haven't failed you yet, have I?"

"No, Jack, you're good." I said as I drew a deep breath. I swallowed uneasily and cleared my throat. "Jack, this engine failure may be directly related to the umbrella effect of electrical interference generated by the spacecraft. The robot may have finished with the East Coast by now and might be headed inland toward the mid-west. I'm afraid we may be running out of flying time."

"We should have a visual on Nellis in the next fifteen minutes, Doc. Just hold on tight, we'll make it to area 1."

I had visited Nellis Air Force Base on several occasions and knew area 1 is where the main landing strip and mission support functions are situated. Nellis Air Force Base was named for First Lieutenant William Harrel Nellis, a one-time resident of Las Vegas, and P-47 fighter pilot who lost his life in the Battle of the Bulge in 1944. B-17 and B-29 gunnery practice was a top priority at the base during the war years. I also knew the air base was in very close proximity to Las Vegas. As a matter of fact, area 3, where base housing exists, is directly across Las Vegas Boulevard from area 1. Area 2 is where all munitions for the base is stored and would be a primary target for Gort to destroy. It was on the outer perimeters of area 2 that I planned to intercept the robot.

I hastily tried to cover all the possibilities in my mind. It was then that I had remembered reading the base was spread out over 11,300 acres. And if I remembered correctly, at the end of 2011, quite a bit, roughly 60 percent, of those 11,300 acres were still relatively undeveloped. I had hoped to use this fact to my advantage by staging my interception of the robot in an undeveloped perimeter area of the base.

Having experienced a distinct sensation that the aircraft had suddenly began descending, I could not resist an effort to peer down at the earth rising up to meet us. I could see some pretty mountainous terrain in front of us as well and definitely felt a large concern rising within me. I had hoped to never experience the feeling of riding in an aircraft forty thousand feet without the luxury of hearing some powerful jet engines propelling us toward our destination. Since this event had just happened, I found myself listening intently to the hum of the engines. My panic slowly ebbed as the engines droned on.

"Jack?" I said as I tried to collect myself from disastrous thoughts and images.

"Yeah, Doc, go ahead."

"Are we going to have enough altitude to get over that mountain range in front of us?"

"Won't have to, Doc, we are going to be making a small bank to the left here shortly, which will take us away from that mountainous area. As a matter of fact, we should just be skirting over the tail end of it. We are approaching Nellis and should be able to have visual contact with the base in about five minutes or so. Looks like we are going to have enough engine power to get at least one good shot at a landing on a nice smooth runway. So try not to worry too much, Doc. All systems are running at 100 percent capacity."

"Roger that," I replied as his words had a very soothing reassuring effect on me. "Thanks, Jack. Anything else I should know?"

"Yes. If something should happen in the next few minutes, and I tell you to eject, you press the red-colored ejector device immediately. Do not wait. We may be in a position of critical altitude to bail out. I won't call it unless it is completely necessary."

"Jack, with a catastrophic power failure . . . with all electrical power out . . . the ejection mechanism probably won't fire. So the truth is, we both may have to ride this bird down."

"If that is the case, I will land my aircraft, Doc," Major Holloway stated confidently. "Don't worry, I will get you to where you need to go. As a matter of fact, we should be able to get a visual sighting of Nellis and Las Vegas about now. Yes, there it is, Doc. Can you see it? About 11 o'clock."

"Roger that, Jack. I see it. As soon as we land, I would suggest you get with the commanding officer of the base and have him order a base-wide evacuation order. Since I am acting directly under orders from the president, you can let the commanding officer know those evacuation orders are coming straight from the president. Try and get as many people as far away from this base as possible. I am hoping an order has already been issued concerning Las Vegas being evacuated. And, Jack, since no vehicles are going to be able to move, bicycles or horseback would be a preferred method of locomotion. Those mountains behind the city of Las Vegas should offer ideal concealment and safety if you get to them in time. We may only have a couple of hours before things really get bad around here. I cannot state, with any reasonable factor of certainty, anything about what forces the surrounding areas in proximity to the spacecraft are going to be subjected to. Early analysis indicates surrounding areas may be subjected to lethal radiation and extreme gravitational forces. However, at this time, the absolute truth is . . . we just don't know."

"Well, if that is the case," replied Major Holloway as he performed another small bank to the left, his voice showing a growing concern for my safety, "what the hell do you think is going to keep you alive when you get close enough to confront the robot. Just being within a thousand yards of the robot could be fatal."

"Jack, haven't I asked you not to bore me with minor details," I said as I tried to joke those very same thoughts away from my mind. Truth is, I had been so busy trying to put some type of plan together just to get close to Gort, I had not had much of an opportunity to think about any side effects of being in a near proximity to the robot.

In 1951, when Gort had originally visited our planet, there was no such need to worry about being in close proximity to the robot, unless he was in attack mode. At that time, Klaatu and Gort were visiting Earth in an emissary or diplomatic mode. This visit . . . this trip to Earth was completely different. The spaceship and the robot were both fully in attack mode. Both could have significant defense mechanisms in play to prevent any type of action. However, the knowledge they possessed of our capabilities, coupled with their own superior technology, the actual defense of the ship and robot were probably not a foremost concern of theirs. The intelligence gathered by the alien forces on our planet would have been complete and accurate to the smallest detail. The beings of this Association of Planets, which were responsible for sending Gort on his mission to Earth, would know exactly what we would be capable of in defense of our planet. There seemed to be very little for them to worry about. They knew the technological superiority they possessed would render useless what little resistance we could put up against them.

"All seriousness aside, Doc, what the hell are you going to do when the robot nears your position?" responded Major Holloway in a tight, sour voice to the joking aspect of my comment.

"If I knew that, Jack, I would feel a lot better about the whole process. All I have figured out is that I need to be within speaking distance of the robot. I am gambling everything on the calculation of one, he recognizes me and/or my voice, and two, Gort will respond in a positive manner to the few sentences or phrases I have at my command in my attempt to try and communicate with the robot. I must be close, very close, to the robot. Therein lies the rub. I am going to be standing defenseless in front of the most lethal force this planet has ever known. Like I explained to the president, I'm only going to get one chance at this. I have to make the most of it. God, I just hope I don't freeze up at a critical moment. You know, Jack, I think there exists a very great probability of me being . . . scared shitless."

"Need a helper, Doc?" asked Jack in a very sincere and honest manner. His voice remained steady, calm, and confident.

"No, thanks." I answered without a second thought, "I'm grateful for the offer, Jack, but you just concentrate on getting you and your wife to safety. Save as many people on the base as you can. It will be better if I deal with this malevolent force on my own, and in my own way. If my calculations are correct, I should be able to handle this myself. If my calculations are incorrect, then there is really no logic in getting us both killed."

"All right. Whatever you say, Doc. There is Nellis Air Force Base and Las Vegas coming into view straight ahead of us," Major Holloway stated.

"Stand by for landing. Oh, and Doc, if I can ever be of any help in any way, don't hesitate to call me."

I could clearly make out the well-defined areas of the rapidly approaching runway. There was no other air traffic to be seen, which is highly unusual for Nellis Air Force Base, since it is home to many different squadrons, including some international ones as well. With the runway coming up to meet us, I mentally prepared myself for the small jolt awaiting as we touched back down upon this once sweet Earth.

I knew I had very little time left before I would find myself face to face with Gort. I felt a very queasy feeling in the pit of my stomach and realized my mouth was bone-dry. As I unhooked the oxygen mask from my face, I was forced to wipe my brow clean of the accumulated sweat. I rubbed my eyes, and stared down at the ground and watched with great interest as the ground rose to meet us until there was the familiar bump as our landing gear made its way into the down and locked position. It was only a matter of a few seconds until I felt the familiar bump of the aircraft touching down.

As I watched with strong interest, Jack taxied the F-22 to what could turn out to be its final resting place. The Plexiglas canopy slid back into the open cockpit position. With a quick and incredible efficiency, two very young-looking airman rushed a small, compact ladder to the side of our aircraft. Climbing shakily out of the F-22, my legs nearly faltered as I touched the earth. I made a point of pausing a few precious seconds to catch my breath and control my breathing. Major Holloway made his way over to me.

"You all right, Doc?"

"Never felt better, Jack," I lied unconvincingly.

"We better make our way over to the operations room and get out of our flight suits."

Chapter Nine

Meet Mr. Gort

0710
22 Dec 2012
Nellis Air Force Base

After grabbing a quick sandwich on the way into the operations room, both Major Holloway and I were met by the commanding officer as we walked into the alcove. Major Holloway made the introductions and explained my mission. In a straightforward manner, Jack made it crystal-clear I was here at the command of the president of the United States. The general, with eyes blinking, cheeks blazing, finally led us to a conference table. He gestured irritably, waving us toward our proposed seats. General Theodore "Ted" Hawkins was possessed of broad shoulders and a slim athletic build. His short-cropped hair betrayed some small semblance of Gray. He stood roughly six feet tall and wore basic black glasses that somehow seemed to complement his rugged square jaw rather well. There could be no mistaking this is one man who was not at all happy with my presence on his air base.

"Dr. Benson," began the general, "I had a quick conference call with the president of the United States about an hour ago before all lines of communication went dead. He ordered me to give you my fullest cooperation and to give you a brief update on the crisis."

"Thank you, General," I said as I leaned back slightly in my chair. I was beginning to feel dead tired once again. The exhilaration of the flight had worn off, and my mission was weighing heavily upon me.

"We lost all communication sometime ago as well, so what is the current situation, General?"

"Complete and utter disaster," stated General Hawkins simply. "Every nuclear facility, every military base, every large city on the East Coast has simply disappeared, vaporized in a matter of seconds. The only thing left standing is a pile of molten metal and scorched earth. We also had intelligence that stated every American, Russian, and British nuclear submarine on patrol in the Atlantic has been presumably destroyed. Millions of dead fish and other sea life have reportedly been washing up on our East Coast. Anything or anyone coming within miles of the spaceship has been cooked. Apparently, our military forces had attempted to intercept the spaceship around the area of Oak Ridge, Tennessee, the site of the old Oak Ridge National Laboratory. These intercepting forces had no chance. Hell, they did not even get the chance to fire a shot in their defense. They were wiped out with 100 percent fatalities! The whole of the country east of the Mississippi has no electrical energy capability whatsoever. There is a total blackout on that side of the country . . . nothing going in, nothing getting out. Casualties are already reaching into the high millions."

"Damn," uttered Major Holloway as he closed his eyes and shook his head.

"Sometimes the damage was completed from the spaceship itself, and other times the robot disembarked from the ship and did the dastardly deed," continued the general. "There doesn't seem to be a pattern of when or why the robot executes the devastation or when the spaceship does the destruction. Anyway, another interception attempt is being arranged at this time. The appointed forces will try to stop the spaceship somewhere on this side of the Mississippi. If this attack fails as well, then the western part of the United States will be rendered open to destruction. The president has ordered me and all other area commanders not to attempt any attack on the spaceship or the robot should this impending attack at the Mississippi fail. Damn it! We are ordered to stand idly by and watch our country be destroyed. I never thought in my military career I would ever receive orders along those lines."

"Unfortunately, General, those are most appropriate orders. Under the present circumstances, General, there is not much else we can do. No technology we have can penetrate the defenses of either the spaceship or the robot," I stated flatly. "The best thing you can do is evacuate this base immediately. Get as many of your people as far from this base as possible," I replied urgently as I drew a deep breath.

"The president ordered me not to intercept the threat, Dr. Benson," scowled the general, righteous and indignant, as he stared me squarely in the eyes, "He did not order me to quit my post!"

"General," I answered him as firmly and resolutely as he had spoken to me, "on behalf of the president of the United States of America, I am hereby giving you that order. And I expect it to be carried out immediately! If you and your people stay, you will all die uselessly. There is no way to stop this force . . . nothing you can do. I will not allow you to sacrifice the good men and women under your command for nothing. Know that I am speaking with the full authority of the president of the United States. I am giving you the order to evacuate this base immediately!"

"Begging your pardon, Dr. Benson, but you do not understand what you are ordering me to do," replied the general dramatically as he stood up, towering over me. I did not appreciate the attempt to intimidate me. I was tired and irritated, and I fired right back at him.

"On the contrary, General, I know exactly what I am doing! I am saving the lives of your men and women. We are going to need good men and women like these to help restore order and rebuild our country in the future. I repeat my order, General," I said firmly., as I suddenly sprang to my feet. I was eyeball to eyeball with the general.

"Issue the order to evacuate this base immediately!" I said with grave determination.

The general seemed to finally realize the futility of his argument and backed down. With what must have been a supreme effort to calm himself, he drew back convulsively. The general suddenly looked completely crestfallen. It was understandable. In light of the distinct aversion he felt toward those orders, it was completely understandable that he looked as sad as he did. This was an order that no military man ever wanted to give. In his mind, I was positive he thought he was abandoning his post . . . running away from a fight . . . surrendering.

However, it was now incumbent upon me not to allow his military thinking to lead to the death those thousands of good men and women that he commanded. The general drew a cigar out of his coat pocket and lazily lit it. Eyeing me suspiciously, he reluctantly picked up the red telephone on the conference table, pressed two numbers, and spoke.

"XO, this is General Hawkins. For immediate action: issue the order to evacuate the base. Have individual section chiefs set primary and secondary rendezvous points according to plans. I want this base empty in thirty minutes . . . CO out," said the general in an angry and resigned tone of voice. If he wanted this base evacuated in thirty minutes, my bet is that he would be able to make it happen in twenty-nine minutes.

"Anything else, Dr. Benson," asked General Hawkins scathingly as he slammed down the telephone receiver into its cradle.

"Just a bicycle to get me where I need to be. I must station myself to intercept the robot," I replied as I moved away from the conference table.

"And where will that be?" asked the general as he proceeded to escort me to the door of the operations room.

"Somewhere on the east perimeter of the base," I replied in a matter-of-fact tone of voice. "I want to be far enough from the center of the base to be able to intercept the robot after the spaceship lands. With any luck, I will stop the robot before he begins attacking your air base, General. My placement and timing are going to have to be impeccable, or I am toast."

"Well, good luck, Dr. Benson. I have got to see to the evacuation of the base," said the general as he stuck out his hand to shake mine. I grasped his hand firmly and reciprocated the handshake. The animosity had all but vanished. The general seemed sincere in his wishes to me.

"Good luck to you too, General. Good luck to us all," I replied sincerely. I turned to Major Holloway. "Jack, once again, thanks and good luck. Godspeed to you and your wife. I hope the end of the day finds you both safe and good.

"Thanks, Doc. Good luck and God bless you," replied Major Holloway as he shook my hand for the last time.

I watched in sadness as he turned and strode out through the door of the operations room. I thought this would be the last time I would probably ever see him again. I stood grim and dismayed as I shook those melancholy thoughts from my mind. I resolutely followed Major Holloway out of the door. I glanced up at the sky as I walked back out into the warm morning sunshine. In the nearby distance, I could see an airman riding a bicycle toward me. A more profound disquiet possessed me as I stopped and waited. The general, good to his word, as I knew he would be, was having my mode of transportation delivered.

As I looked around, I could see all types of scattered activity taking place with accelerated purpose. There was a flurry of movement taking place in every direction I looked. It was all foot traffic, however, as the electrical dampening effect preceding the attacks had started to take place. No cars, trucks, or aircraft were moving whatsoever. I could almost visualize this base being totally vacated and empty, looking like some sort of ghost town. As the airman drew close, he jumped off the bike, approached me on foot, and saluted. He looked to be all of eighteen years old, his face lined with worry and whitened by fear.

"Thanks, son," I said as I took control of the bike from him. "Now get yourself the hell out of here."

"Yes, sir!" he shouted excitably in response and abruptly turned and ran off to join the rest of his unit in evacuating the base. I smiled as I momentarily watched him jog his way back to his friends who were gathered in a tight group waiting for him. They all turned in unison as he joined them and jogged away toward their destination.

I breathed a deep sigh and turned my attention to what I knew I needed to do. Fear was steadily working up my spine as I climbed aboard the bicycle. I started pedaling my way slowly out to the eastern perimeter of the base. A sudden sense of futility gripped me as I was searching for some area that could afford a measure of concealment. Trying to quiet the terror within me, I began to focus my thoughts on the type of concealment that could be most practical. I really had no idea what type of concealment would be afforded me, but I was hoping for the best.

As I continued my pedaling, I could discern a noticeable decrease in activity as the base was emptying out at a fairly rapid pace. In about ten minutes I would be the only one left on base. I was praying Major Holloway and his wife would be far from this area before Gort arrived. I desperately wanted everyone as far from the target area as possible, as I knew this base would be hammered by catastrophe. I had been informed upon my arrival that Las Vegas was being evacuated as well. I knew once Gort was finished with his work in this area, there would be no MGM Grand, no Mirage, no Treasure Island or Bellagio, or all the rest. If they wanted a supercasino city in the middle of a desert, they would have to completely rebuild. The only hope for Las Vegas was if I could somehow communicate with Gort and halt this mission of destruction. The chance surely existed, but I wouldn't want to bet the odds on it.

As I finally approached the perimeter of the east sector of Nellis Air Force Base, I could see the desert rise up to meet the edge of the concrete, shimmering in the morning sun. Upon first inspection, there didn't seem to be much in the form of concealment. I rode to the right for a few minutes and found nothing. I turned and rode back to the left edge of the runway. It was then to my surprise and delight, I stumbled upon a small metal hatchway complete with a rusty handle, located on the edge of the runway. I got off my bike and slowly lifted up the door. The inside space was small and compact, about three feet deep by four feet wide in the form of a square. I had no idea what this was originally designed for, but I could only suppose it was some sort of storage place for tools or parts. It was immediately evident, this place had been abandoned and left unused for years.

I began to wonder if anyone even remembered this space was here. Chances were this whole area had remained untouched since World War II. I slowly lowered myself down inside the small underground storage space.

Once inside, I grabbed the hatch and lowered it back down into place behind me. It was cool and dry inside the cramped confines of the hole. When the hatch was securely shut, total darkness enveloped me. The choice required scarcely a thought. This was it! However, it wasn't very long until I began to immensely dislike the feeling of being enclosed in such a small space with no form of light. There was a definite claustrophobic chill running the length of my spine, so I rapidly lifted the hatch and stood up. The warm sun on my face was a welcome relief. Although it was the desert in December, the day was turning out to be blessedly warm and sunny. The ambient temperature must have been around sixty-five degrees, and the desert wind blew small and faint. As I glanced skyward and realized there was nothing but clear blue sky above me, I began to feel a little more confident.

Looking at my watch, which was of the old-fashioned, wind-up variety, the time was 0818. There was no distinct and sure way of knowing when the spaceship might arrive, but I could, in my mind's eye, imagine the spaceship hovering momentarily motionless over all the minutemen missile silos secretly located in Oklahoma, Nebraska, Kansas, and all the way up to South Dakota and North Dakota. Then, in a blinding flash of energy, destroying every single missile silo in sight.

I have no doubt the advanced technology possessed by the Association of Planets, which had sent Gort aboard the spaceship to destroy all nuclear capabilities on Earth, would have had no trouble at all in being able to gather intelligence about our defenses from our defense computer network. I am sure it had managed to do that in China, North Korea, Russia, and the rest of the nations it attacked. Hell, it probably received a lion's share of information from the Internet as well! I can only hope the order was issued to abandon those military sites, as well as all others, in time to spare the lives of those manning their positions. If not, those remaining at their stations inside the targeted missile silos would be cooked alive, or vaporized, in the ensuing explosion from the powerful energy beam directed by either the ship or the robot.

I was growing very weary of thinking of all the possible catastrophes that might befall everyone in the United States. Truth is, I was just growing weary. I suddenly felt so sleepy. My eyelids were growing heavier. As I lay inside the hatch with the door open, sun shining warmly on my face, I realized sleep had, once again, become such a precious commodity. Slowly hypnotized by the warmth of the sun and the sounds of the desert and the peaceful vastness, I slowly drifted off into wonderful oblivion . . .

Humming. A very low humming sound at first began to rouse me from my sleep. My muscles felt cramped and sore as there had not been much room to stretch out within the confines of my hideaway. With the hatch open, I could definitely hear the humming sound begin to grow in intensity. It wasn't long until I also became aware of a very unusual and uncomfortable feeling creeping up the length of my body. It was a very singular tingling sensation. One with a bit of a bite to it! The feeling was highly irritating and uncomfortable. It was eerily like the sensation of being pinched all over my body. That tingling and pinching sensation began to, little by little, grow in intensity. It seemed to parallel the growing intensity of the humming sound.

The sudden sensations worked to heighten my curiosity, and in an act of irrational impatience, I slowly stood up in the hatchway. As I scanned the horizon, I could see nothing unusual or imminent, just the cool, smooth desert sands meeting the clear blue sky somewhere off in the distance. I hazarded a quick glance at my watch. The time was 0952. I must have dozed off for an hour or so at the most. I refocused my attentions toward the plains to the east of my position. The sun was partly obscuring my vision, and even with my high-definition sunglasses on, the viewing was rendered difficult. Nervously awaiting for the events to come, miles off in the distance, I could begin to perceive the faint outline of the saucer-shaped spaceship hovering low over the ground. The ship was moving slowly, almost rhythmically. It sparkled and glittered in the clear desert sunlight. The startling and intense brilliancy of the spaceship instantly created within me a spirit of wonder and perplexity. From the uttermost regions of deep space, this specter precipitously produced a simultaneous sentiment of deep awe and foreboding. It was at this time I felt the full impact of my perilous position.

I began hyperventilating. I fought to control my breathing. I felt an irrepressible urge to just get the hell out of this coffinlike chamber and make a run for it. But run to where? There was certainly no safe place to run.

There soon began a small sensation of burning on my skin, which accompanied the itching and pinching feelings pummeling my body. I noticed I was profusely sweating as well. There was no speculation necessary; I could undeniably feel the increase in temperature accompanying the spacecraft as it neared my position. The heat was becoming unbearable as the ship neared. This rise in temperature was making it very difficult to concentrate. I watched in mixed horror and fascination as the ship slowly approached from the east. Gravitational laws did not seem to affect this ship whatsoever. It leisurely floated closer and closer to the base, yet it must have taken only a few seconds to approach. It was as if time was distorted within the spherical influence of the spaceship.

Abruptly, the heat dissipated, and a sudden silence descended all around me. It was then I realized I was now inside the sphere of electrical interference, almost like being in the eye of a hurricane. The ship slowly began a rapid but controlled descent, until it was set down upon the earth. Once the spacecraft had landed, the sensations plaguing my body had totally subsided. It was only a few moments after it came to rest that an opening began to appear on the hull of the ship. As the top portion, or the dome, of the ship slowly opened to the right, a long metal walkway simultaneously began to slide forward from the interior of the ship. The extended walkway declined to the earth at a steep angle. An able-bodied person would have no trouble ascending the ramp, but its steepness appeared to be too much for anyone with a handicap. I slowly lowered myself down into the hatchway and covered myself with the lid. I allowed a slight crack to remain open and peered intensely through it at the terrifying sight before me.

I have never been a man of great eloquence, so my original observations of the robot may not do the reader of this account descriptive justice. But I shall try my best to relay an accurate image of what my eyes recorded.

Gort began his inexorable walk out from the depths of the ship much in the same manner I had originally observed him move in 1951. Each step seemed precise and methodical in nature. The robot moved with relentless determination. There was no wasted movement, just the exact, mechanized movement of an automated being. The sun was reflecting a brilliant aura off his metallic, silver body.

Gort was as large and menacing as I had originally remembered. The robot continued down the walkway, and once the robot stood on firm ground, I watched in fascination as the walkway began to disappear back inside the hull of the ship. The opening on the saucer's dome was once again shut, and nowhere could a seam be found on the hull of the spaceship. It was of perfect shape once again. Gort began his deliberate walk toward the eastern perimeter of Nellis Air Force Base. I could not have asked for better luck as the robot was a scant thirty yards from me, and the spaceship a mere five more from my position. So far, the universe was with me!

I tried unsuccessfully to suppress a shudder of intense fear from flowing through my body as Gort, step by step, approached my tomblike hole in the ground. I had the hatch lifted only a few inches for my observations of the proceedings, but apparently that was a few inches too many. Gort's head slowly, almost imperceptibly turned toward my position. The robot turned and altered his stride slightly in my direction. Gort had began to approach my exact location. Whether the robot could "see" or whether he could sense me, I supposed I would never know. What was painfully obvious to me, there could be no mistake . . . the robot was walking directly toward my position. I wanted to run, to scream, to shout, to do something, anything! I fought fear for control of my body! I knew my position had been compromised, and there was nothing I could do about it.

Gort had now approached to within approximately fifteen feet of me. There was nothing else to do but to stand up and prepare for the inevitable confrontation. I felt as if my body had been thrown into a wild state of confusion. My legs wobbled and trembled fiercely as I stood up and threw the hatch back. As I shakily climbed up out of the hole, I kept my eyes on Gort as he inched closer to me. I managed a few hesitant steps toward the robot.

It was within roughly ten feet of me that Gort's metal visor began to slowly rise. I marveled at the intense, brilliant, white light, sparkling, rotating, pulsing in the glasslike, enclosed, yet mysteriously opaque area where the visor once rested. I was on the verge of becoming mesmerized by the beautiful and intriguing sight of the pulsating light within the glass visor of the robot. Gort now stood within six feet of me. The robot towered over me, leaning its upper torso menacingly toward me. The thought struck me that I was only a second or two from being vaporized into the seemingly nothingness of death. I prodded myself to action.

"Gort! *Declanto Rosco!*" I shouted toward the robot. My words echoed in my ears and seemed weak. The pulsating light continued to sparkle within the helmet of the robot. The hypnotizing light seemed to have taken on some type of rotational momentum.

"Gort! *Declanto Rosco*," I repeated, this time with much more force. The fact I was still alive at that moment was an encouraging event. Obviously, what I said had some type of effect upon the robot. Gort had come to a virtual halt. I boldly decided to try my luck a little more.

"Gort, *Barrada Nictoe. Meringa.*"

Gort's visor slowly lowered until the brilliant pulsating light was extinguished from the robot's face. My commands to the robot had apparently been recognized and acted upon. Gort slowly moved toward me and, with little or no effort, scooped me up, limp as a rag doll, into his metallic arms. The robot turned slowly and began to carry me back toward the spaceship. My heart was beating so ferociously; I felt as if it was ready to burst within me. I did not resist any action by Gort but had instantly become a willing, compliant subject. There was nothing I could do at this point to resist such a force anyway.

As we neared the spaceship, I could see the walkway glide out to meet us and the dome of the ship open as it had before. Once reaching the walkway, Gort continued up the platform and into the interior of the ship. I turned my head and watched in horrible fascination as the opening closed silently behind us. I was now inside the spaceship!

The spaceship was much as my mother had described it in her writings. The similarities were quite unmistakable. I could recognize many of the things she described about the inner hull and the interior walkway circling the outer part of the ship. As was the case with her, I could not discern any connecting seams or entranceways into the inner part of the ship until we were apparently standing in front of one. The seam to the door only appeared the moment before it began to open. The hallway was well lit, and I could see the panels with the horizontal slits mother had described in her original account concerning the interior of the ship. All the fear seemed to have left my mind. I was now consumed with an overwhelming curiosity about everything I could observe in the ship's interior. My scientific mind had wrested control back from the fearful part of my mind.

The metal comprising the hull of the ship was exactly as mother described as to the transparency aspect! I could actually see outside the ship simply by looking through the hull. Yet I knew the hull was composed of the strongest possible metal alloy, quite alien to any metal on earth. I gasped half in terror, half in excitement as the entranceway to the interior of the ship silently opened before us. Gort carried me inside.

I watched the door close behind us and, once again, could not discern a seam to indicate any kind of doorway that had previously existed. My eyes instantly riveted to what mother described as the large communication screen. It was still exactly as she had described it years ago. But then, as I gained a chance to observe more closely, there were apparently a few new features added. I had no idea what the intended application of these features were. Then again, I had no idea what the original features were used for either.

I moved my attention to the large gyroscopic feature in the center of the room. It was spinning slowly and would continue to do so throughout my stay aboard the spacecraft. I calculated the gyroscope completed about one revolution every thirty seconds or so. My second impression was that this device may be part of what kept the ship afloat so effortlessly in the Earth's gravity. It was then that another thought struck me. I recalled as the ship had landed near my position, I did not notice any desert dust being kicked up from the ground upon which it landed. There was a strong humming sound and the awful sensation upon my skin, but no sign of any thrust of air exiting the undersection of the craft. This spaceship was somehow able to defy the laws of gravity associated with our planet!

As Gort continued to carry me across the inner chamber of the ship, I could clearly see how absolutely correct and accurate my mother's description of the inside of the spaceship turned out to be. She most definitely possessed a clear eye for details. I quickly surmised whoever built this spacecraft had a strict adherence to the essentials. There seem to be no item of comfort whatsoever aboard the ship. There, also, was no other being aboard the ship. Gort apparently had received his orders from the Association of Planets and had been previously programmed to carry them out as specified without any further direction from an accompanying being. If he was receiving any updated information, it was exclusively through the communication device within the ship.

I had hoped there would be a live being aboard the ship I could communicate with in an attempt to stop this destruction of our planet. Unfortunately, this was not to be the case. My ability to communicate with Gort was, of course, severely limited. There existed the possibility the robot could have been programmed to understand the English language. Gort may have been programmed to understand many different languages. Since our planet and its inhabitants had been studied for generations, the creators of Gort may have input some data concerning our language into his memory banks. I immediately deemed it worth a try, so I looked to Gort and spoke.

"Gort, I am Robert Benson, you remember, little Bobby Benson. It was many years ago we met. I was a friend of Klaatu. I knew Klaatu! Gort, you may put me down now!" I stated, hoping the name Klaatu would have some visible effect on the robot. "Gort, you must have received programming or updated data concerning my face and/or my voice!'

My words had no visible effect on the robot. Gort had fully crossed the interior of the ship. I had turned my head in an effort to see where we had stopped and instantly recognized the sleeping chamber that mother described in vividly accurate details. This was the very chamber in which Klaatu had lain while being brought back to life after he had been shot and killed by the army. It was merely an uncomfortable-looking platform with some type of headrest. Behind the headrest was a small glassed-in, circular chamber, which was lit with alternating pulsing beams of multicolored lights. It was both beautiful and fascinating. I turned my attention back to the robot and again attempted to communicate with it.

"Gort, Klaatu *imray narawak . . .*"

Gort did not respond to word or phrase. The robot extended his arms and began to gently lower me down into position on the platform. I at once began to struggle to get to my feet, but Gort methodically held me down to the platform with one large, cold metal hand, while he leisurely moved his other hand over the top portion of my body and across my head. As he did so, I lost the ability to struggle. An unanticipated calm along with a soothing, quiet sensation began flowing through my body. I had lost the will to struggle and move! However, I did not seem to mind in the least. My mind seemed to be empty of all dreadful and fear-inspiring thoughts. I was not harmed in any way, just feeling a very peaceful presence coursing throughout my body. It was as though I lay hypnotized from physical action, but my mind was alert, attentive, and capable of processing thoughts and staying active. All my muscles relaxed. I was breathing deeply and easily.

Once the robot had quieted me, he stood up, towering above me, as though he was benevolently looking down upon me. Gort turned and waved his hand in front of a small row of lights. The lights began to flash in a more rapid manner. I could feel a small sensation of odorless air flowing leisurely over the length of my body. Since I could not distinguish any odor of any type associated with the flow of air, I found myself at a loss to determine whether this was a type of gas. I marveled at the technology, as I could not see any type of Plexiglas covering over me but could definitely feel a sense of being encased in some form of material.

I wanted to speak but could not. I could not move my lips or any other portion of my body. My eyes were opened but not moving well at all. In fact, my eyelids were becoming very difficult to keep open. The effect of the unknown vapor was readily apparently . . . I had lost all ability to move any set of muscles in my body. In my peripheral vision, I could see Gort perform some sort of gradual motion with his hand once again. This time I could definitely sense a small gust of air or odorless gas flow across my face. It was much more pronounced. My eyelids were becoming more heavy. Struggle as I might, I could not keep them open. I thought to myself, "I must not fall asleep . . . I must not fall . . ."

Chapter Ten

Moori

Unknown Time
Unknown Date
Unknown Location

I came to consciousness with a start and could feel my head slightly swirling. I endeavored to open my eyes. The sensation was not an unpleasant feeling; it was just something I had never experienced before in my life. As my eyes opened at a very relaxed and unhurried pace, I could scarcely perceive the large, silvery, metallic form of the robot standing over me. I watched with piqued interest as the robot, with slow deliberation, raise his arm and then in one smooth motion, pass his hand over a small row of pulsating lights. A small gust of what I can only describe as a springtime-freshness smell misted across my face. I at once began to feel much invigorated, and my ability to think, reason, and move seemed to be gradually returning to my body. As I mentally took measure of my mind and body, there seemed to be no ill side effect of what I had experienced.

I had no idea how long I had been in this state of induced hibernation, nor had I any real idea of my current location, other than still being inside the spaceship. All I knew for certain at this point was . . . I still seemed be under the control of the robot. It was wholly beyond my powers to sense any type of movement of the spaceship, so I did not know if we were on Earth or had ascended into space. As history records, it turned out neither of my assumptions were correct.

I gradually managed to sit in an upright position on the sleep platform, and seemed I did so without the sensation of expending much effort or energy. I happily found myself to be without any residual sluggishness from the hibernation period. Beginning to feel relatively refreshed, I took a couple of deep breaths. I watched in curiosity as the robot moved away from me then stood motionless.

I carefully stood up, fearing my legs would be very wobbly and unable to initially support my weight. Ultimately, to my very pleasant surprise, my legs felt as good and strong as the rest of my body had upon awakening. Inconceivably, there seemed to be no aftereffects of my deep sleep in any form. I once again breathed in deeply, and even this small, refreshing act seemed to be accomplished more easily than ever before in my life. In fact, as I thought about it, I hadn't felt this energized and invigorated since I was about thirty years old! I was experiencing a truly remarkable feeling! The only problem I could sense was that my vision was a little blurred. I slowly took off my glasses to inspect them and instantly noticed my vision cleared up. Having no satisfactory explanation for it, I seemingly had somehow regained the ability to see without the use of my glasses. It was as if my eyes had been healed completely. I would venture to say my eyesight had been corrected to slightly stronger than 20/20 vision. Something astonishing . . . something wonderful had occurred while I was in the sleep chamber. I seemed to have been cured of all the maladies that come with aging!

"I have got to get me one of those," I said aloud as I looked at Gort. The robot remained motionless against the inner wall, next to the communication device.

I began to carefully move around the inside chamber of the ship, studying everything I could see. I wanted to absorb as much as I could while I had the chance.

Gort remained motionless only for a moment longer. The robot suddenly began to walk toward another vertical chamber stationed against the interior wall of the structure. I had not noticed this second chamber when first brought aboard the spaceship. I could not be sure, but I do not think the chamber was visible upon my initial inspection of the control room. Gort strode to the front of the cell, turned, and backed slowly toward the wall. Once against the wall, he, again, became motionless. I stood and stared at the robot for a few moments then made my way toward where he was stationed. I thought I would try and determine if the robot was in rest mode or somehow had shut completely down.

"Gort," I said simply as I started to turn and walk away. "*Meringa!*"

I did not know if the robot would follow me, as I believed the command "*meringa*" asked him to do, or whether the robot would remain still. Gort had become part of the wall of the ship. The robot did not move. The robot either did not recognize my command or was completely shut down. I stopped, turned, and faced the robot once again. I stared intently at Gort. With a mixture of relief and displeasure, I had begun to consider that I had been dreadfully disillusioned in thinking I had somehow communicated with the robot.

"Gort!" I snorted indignantly, not expecting any response from the robot. "Will you please tell me . . . where the hell are we?"

"You are on my home planet, the planet we call Muurae," came a light and feathery female voice from directly behind and opposite me. It sounded as if it came from outside of the chamber. I whirled quickly around and found myself face to face with a beautiful woman, appearing to be about thirty-five years old. She had long black hair, beautiful black eyes, and long, sharp nose with a cute little mouth. Her body seemed perfectly proportioned for her five-foot-ten-inch frame. She possessed a lovely smile and a vibrant personality, which was at once enthusiastic and full of an infectious charm. Dressed in a one-piece, bright yellow jumpsuit, she was quite the sight. My confusion was complete, and I readily admit I was stunned beyond belief. And that was putting it mildly! My blank stare of absolute bewilderment must have slightly amused her. She smiled at me sweetly and advanced toward me.

"I am Moori," she stated in a light, lovely voice, quickening her pace toward me. "Daughter of Koori and Klaatu. I believe you know my father. He speaks very fondly of you and has told me many stories of the time you spent together."

"Daughter of Klaatu . . . ?" I stammered, betraying my confusion at the new set of circumstances facing me. I took a few hesitant and shaky steps forward. I was desperately trying to quiet the mounting confusion within me.

"Yes, Dr. Benson. I am Klaatu's daughter. He has asked that I greet you and accompany you to our residential habitat. I believe you call it a . . . home."

"Yes, of course. I would be delighted," I replied as I blinked then shut my eyes. Was this a dream? I opened my eyes slowly. Moori was still there.

"Excellent," she replied promptly. "Please allow me to escort you, Dr. Benson.

"Please, call me Robert."

"Very well, Robert," she said. Moori then gave a little laugh. "I'm afraid my father still calls you . . . Bobby. I guess he still thinks of you as a little boy."

Moori half turned her body back toward the opening from which she entered the inner chamber of the ship. I could see her twist her head around slightly to ensure I was following her. I increased my gait to catch up to her and assumed a position at her right-hand side. She almost immediately entwined her arm within mine, leading me toward the sliding, metal walkway exiting the spaceship. The warmth of her touch and the accompanying genuineness of the act touched me deeply.

"I believe you will find our planet a little different than yours, which should prove to be of some passing interest to you," she stated. With an amiable gesture of her left hand waving my attention toward the splendor of the view unfolding before me, we walked down the pathway out of the ship. A blue-white sun shone brightly against the background of a swirling blue and purplish sky. I could distinctly see three moons in the distance. Two were closer than the third. Moori noticed me looking skyward and spoke.

"Yes, Robert, there are three moons revolving around our planet. Two are inhabited. The distant moon you see is uninhabitable as it consists mostly of barren rock and has an atmosphere of gaseous mists and exploding volcanic masses. It really is quite inhospitable. However, we are able to tap the energy output of that inhospitable moon, providing us with much of the power that we need."

"Fascinating," I responded as I stepped off the metal path and took my first steps on the planet Muurae. Tears came to my eyes as I felt a faint warm swirling wind caress my cheeks. I drew a deep breath and began to observe these alien surroundings. Even though the sun was shining brightly, I could still see some stars shining true and steady in the heavens. Among the missing stars were all the constellations I had studied on Earth. I could not recognize any of the star patterns I observed.

"Where is planet . . . Muurae . . . located, anyway?" I asked as I felt my pulse quickening, my heart pounding. She answered as she steered me toward a small, compact, bug of a car, which seemed to be hovering two feet above the ground. I theorized there must have been some type of magnetic force holding the craft above ground and in place, but I could neither feel, hear, or see anything to prove that assumption to be correct.

In the distance, I could see pillars of rocks, sparkling with gold and silver in the sunlight. There also seem to be a variety of crystalline pillars, each surrounded by its own swirling mist. A ghostly radiance reflected all around me. My first impression was this was largely a crystalline planet, consisting of sparkling stones, reflecting the light from a nearby sun.

"Our universe is quite some distance from yours. It is a wheel-shaped universe, consisting of many galaxies. Planet Muurae is on a distant rim of one of those galaxies. Our galaxy has roughly a million suns, consisting of many habitable planets. Ours is a civilized galaxy with war having been outlawed for thousands of years," she sighed with a warm, satisfying smile.

We had now stopped and stood next to the bug-car. "Please enter this mechanized transporter which will convey us to our destination," she stated matter-of-factly as the gull-wing door of the vehicle opened automatically. From the outside, the vehicle looked very compact and uncomfortable, but once inside there seem to be ample room. The cockpit of the vehicle was covered by a Plexiglas-type bubble, which allowed for spectacular viewing. The rest of the vehicle seemed to be made of the same metal alloy of which the spaceship had been constructed. As I climbed in the bug-car, I noticed there was no steering wheel or steering device of any type. The interior was roomy, posh, and comfortable. A small square of round pulsing lights, varying in colors, was situated on a small console between our seats. There were no backseats.

I watched anxiously as Moori walked behind the car to the other side. She stepped gracefully into the vehicle, and the doors on both sides of the vehicle closed automatically without a discernable sound. As she adjusted her body down into the plush seat, she tapped one of the lights on the console. The light stopped pulsating and maintained a light green color. The vehicle began to move. However, much to my surprise, there was no immediate sensation of movement.

"As you can see, Robert, much like the planet Earth, we have one sun for our planet. It is slightly larger than your sun. I believe your sun's radius is roughly 432,169 miles and is roughly 93 million miles from Earth. Our sun's radius 505,610 miles and is approximately 107 million miles from Muurae. As a result of all this, we enjoy thirty hours of sunlight followed by seven hours of darkness. I guess this would be what you would term a "day." We usually have it rain at night for two hours to help refresh and sustain our plant life. It may interest you that most of our citizens grow their own vegetables inside their personal solariums."

"Have it rain at night?" I asked with raising incredulity in my voice. "You mean you can control the weather?"

"Within each farm pod, absolutely. We have had an atmospheric control device in place for hundreds of years. We have plenty of sun year-round, we just needed to add water. So we manufacture it. Within each of our farming pods, we can control the moisture necessary for each plant to an exact degree. Farmers in our society are among the most accomplished and prized citizens. Unlike your planet, farmers are highly cherished here. They rotate and replenish their crops with very little effort, and the end result is the people of Muurae are well fed with fresh, wholesome foods. Outside of the pods, our weather is so wonderful year-round, we found we do not need to alter nature. Usually, it is refreshingly sunny with an average temperature of 80 degrees . . . Fahrenheit. Isn't that what your temperature measurement is called?"

"Yes, it is . . . in some parts of our world. In other parts of the world, they use the centigrade scale."

"So the people of planet Earth cannot even agree on a form of measuring outside ambient temperature?" she asked with a sense of bewilderment.

"Pretty much," I responded flatly with an unconcealed tone of disgust and dismay. "But if you have studied our planet's civilizations closely, you will understand that was the least of our problems."

"Yes . . . I'm sorry about what happened to your planet," she said sincerely. "I wish it could have been avoided. I am afraid the council of the Associations of Planets is very strict in their interpretation about security from aggression. I sometimes wish it were not so."

"Moori, I am afraid I have no knowledge of what happened to Earth after Gort . . ."

"Placed you aboard the spaceship?" she finished my sentence for me. "Gort returned to carry out the final stages of his mission. Every facility associated with nuclear weapons, research, or energy production was destroyed. Nuclear submarines, missiles, silos, power plants . . . all destroyed. Many of the surrounding cities were also devastated. The loss of life on planet Earth was estimated to be approximately four billion."

"My god . . ." I stammered with a sharp gasp of indrawn breath. I slumped miserably down into my seat. A severe sense of horror, pain, and extreme loss swept through my body. I suddenly felt a new dimension of remoteness. A kind of mindless disbelief, a numbness, rapidly accompanied the horror of it all. I could feel my head throbbing under the weight of a myriad of mental images . . . destructive, ugly images. I found myself engulfed by a feeling of terror and extreme loneliness. Moori spoke softly, quietly arousing me out of my lethargic state, "We have arrived at our destination, Robert."

"What? Oh, yes . . . I see."

Our magnetic-pulsed vehicle had pulled abruptly up to a saucer-shaped dome house. There were no discernable windows or doorways around the outside wall of the structure. The sun glittered and reflected off the structure of the dome. What appeared to be a small metallic walkway slid out from the interior of the dome-type house to meet us. A swirling cloud of dust drifted slowly by our vehicle.

"Well, we made it safe and sound, Robert," said Moori as she waved her hand over one of the lights on the console. The two doors of the vehicle again opened automatically, silently. As I clambered out of the vehicle, I noticed many of the same type saucer-shaped dome structures dotted throughout the landscape. It seemed each house occupied a space of two or three acres . . . as a lot size. There must have been hundreds of thousands of them scattered throughout the horizon for as far as the eye could see. There seemed to be veins of crystal light glittering inside the tops of each dome, like some shimmering mirage.

I momentarily wondered if I was observing the entire civilization of this planet then sheepishly smiled at the absolute absurdity of the thought. As I glanced skyward, I could faintly make out a luminous whirlpool in the galaxy seemingly frozen in space directly above us. The magnificent beauty of this alien planet was simultaneously strange and fascinating.

Moori had approached me from behind and to my right, and entwined her arm once again with mine and led me to the beginning of the extended walkway. Once we stepped on to the metallic pathway, we stopped our walking. The pathway began to slowly pull us toward the front of the dome. As we continued to move nearer to the structure, I began to show my apprehension. There was no doorway opening up to allow us entry into the domicile! Moori sensed my increasing concern.

"Do not worry, Robert. I wouldn't allow anything to harm you," she said, smiling up at me sweetly.

My lips drew back involuntarily, almost convulsively as we passed effortlessly through a type of force field that was superbly contrived to act as the entrance to the establishment. Once again, there was nothing to indicate anything existed at that particular spot other than a solid metal wall, rendering it almost meaningless to the naked eye. The illusory effect was breathtaking to say the least.

"Well," I said with an effort of bringing back my breathing to an acceptable rate, "you certainly have perfected that particular science."

"And what science is that?" Moori asked quizzically as she turned her head toward me.

"The science of manufacturing doorways out of metal walls where none previously existed."

Moori gave a quick little dry laugh as she pulled me forward into the dome structure. As I began my observations of the interior of the house, I could not help but be struck by the amount and quality of exquisite china and fragile-looking glass placed perfectly throughout the great cavernous room. Most were encased in glass and on beautifully decorated pillars or stands of about four to six feet in height. The floor upon which I found myself standing seemed to be made of very smooth rock, with much resemblance to Earth's marble. There were no windows in the structure, yet I could see through the wall of the structure to the outside environment without any effort whatsoever. It seems the housing units on this planet were made of much the same material as the spaceships. This had the effect of allowing the illumination of the sun to provide much light into every room. And, yet, I must say this effect was not too overpowering at all, as one might expect of a glasshouse. I speculated there must be some invisible filtering system in place.

As I glanced upward, I could see much of the purplish blue sky through the expansive ceiling of the dome. However, it was readily apparent I could not see through the interior walls of the structure, which was ideal for a sense of privacy. There also were ornate carvings and drawings throughout the great room, along with some very interesting yet very comfortable-looking furniture. There was a curved sofa, enclosed chairs in the shape of an egg, where, I later learned, one could be comforted by soothing music while simultaneously viewing whatever four-dimension holographic displays one desired. In the coming days, I immensely enjoyed visiting some of the other planets and civilizations within this galaxy in the closed comfortable confines of these chairs. The interior of the dome structure struck me as being a complete emanation of splendor. The soothing, sugary voice of Moori shook me out of my observations.

"Robert, if you will make yourself comfortable, I will find my father and bring him to greet you. He is more than likely in his laboratory . . . or out doing his gardening," she said with a wry smile. I sat down on one end of the curved sofa and watched with piqued interest as Moori disappeared through the wall to an adjoining room. I swore softly to myself. I was having a hard time assimilating to these strange surroundings, especially having to walk through apparently solid walls. "How the hell do you know where a door is in this place," I thought to myself as I rubbed my eyes. Having my body disappearing into a featureless and sleek wall did seem to astonish and irritate me. The wonderment I had believed thus far, however, more than made up for any irritable feeling I might have.

"This was going to be more than just a momentary wonder," I thought to myself. I was just beginning to scratch the surface of all the remarkable and fascinating aspects of this world. I supposed I had spent only a couple of minutes in my awe-induced stupor when I heard a voice. It was a voice I hadn't heard for what seemed like ages.

"Bobby! Bobby Benson!"

It was Klaatu!

"You don't know how joyful I am to see you," he continued as he strode amicably toward me. The man I had known as Mr. Carpenter during his brief stay on Earth seemed only to have aged slightly since I had last laid my eyes upon him more than fifty years ago! He definitely appeared as regal, thin, and intellectual as he had first appeared on Earth. His demeanor remained essentially as self-assured and calm as I had remembered. His dogged determination and resultant courage in the face of great odds had always impressed me.

"Klaatu!" I cried and then said nothing more as I excitedly sprang to my feet. I approached him at a quickened pace, extending my open hand toward him. I find myself obliged to acknowledge a feeling of a type of dizzying thrill coursing through my body as he grabbed my hand and pulled me toward him for a short but immensely satisfying hug. I must have been staring in awe and blank bewilderment at him, for a smile crept even further across his face.

"Quite an extraordinary turn of events, isn't it, Bobby." he stated in an effort to bring me back toward normality, whatever normal was under these circumstances. Klaatu was staring at me with those piercing, appraising eyes. "And look at you! All grown up into a handsome man. I can see Moori has become quite fond of you as well."

"Yes, sir," I managed to mumble an answer through my mindless disbelief.

"Bobby, I want to express my sincere sympathies for what befell your mother after I left. The notion of your government being so cruel and evil to personally persecute and terrorized your mother to the extent of making her life a living hell after I had departed, well, it did not even cross my mind this would happen," stated Klaatu in a mournful and deadly serious voice. A hint of anger could be observed in the coloring of his face while expressing those thoughts.

"I had hoped you, your family, and your planet would have benefited more from my visit," stated Klaatu in a slightly disillusioned tone of voice.

"Nothing that happened during your visit or after you left was your fault, Klaatu," I replied glumly, but in a steady voice. "Anyway, that happened years ago, and there is nothing either of us can do to change anything. Besides, Klaatu, everything that has happened since your visit to Earth has led directly to my being here on your planet, today. And I am very grateful of that fact, I assure you."

Moori had now rejoined her father, entwining her arm into his. She looked up lovingly toward her father, speaking in a tender voice, "Father, we should not forget our manners, even under the most joyous and extraordinary set of circumstances in which we find ourselves. Robert must have a desire to freshen up and rest a bit. How about it, Robert? A nice hot shower, or perhaps a soothing hot bath in which to soak in after your long journey?"

"I must confess the idea sounds quite marvelous to me," I responded with scarcely a thought. It had been a long time since I last bathed. Yet there was no outward manifestation of appreciable body odor about me. Nor did I feel dirty or unclean in any manner. The sleep chamber aboard the ship must have cleansed me during the long space flight to this planet. Yes, there did seem to exist an unmistakable impression . . . of an infinite distance being traveled. And it must have transpired at an inconceivable speed.

"You are probably hungry as well, Robert?" asked Klaatu as his eyes widened to match his warm smile. Without waiting for an answer, he continued, "Moori will show you to your suite. It is yours for as long as you like. I am genuinely happy to see you, once again. But come. Freshen up and rest awhile. We will talk more later. Moori, please escort our distinguished guest to his room. Robert, when you are finished with the process of refreshing yourself, we shall resume our conversation over a glass of Muuraen wine. Since we were informed of your arrival, Moori has planned a sumptuously prepared feast in your honor."

"Come, Robert," said Moori as she let go of her father's arm and grabbed mine. I smiled wanly as she led me away from her father. There were so many thousands of questions I had to ask Klaatu, but all of them would have to summarily wait until a little later.

"Until later then, sir" I said as I was being escorted toward the far wall of the vast great room. As we neared the wall, I turned to Moori and spoke,

"I swear, Moori, it is going to take me some getting used to walking through solid walls."

She laughed as she replied, "You must feel like a Kordaian owl lost among the missing stars. I guess I can only conjecture and imagine what it would be like visiting your planet, or any other foreign planet."

"You mean you have not traveled out among the stars like your father?" I asked, a sense of incredulity rising within my voice. It seemed both illogical and improbable that Moori should not have explored the deep space regions outside her home planet.

"I'm afraid I have not inherited the driving curiosity of my father," she replied with a shrug of her soft shoulders. "I guess I am more like my mother in the aspect of being content while occupying ourselves with the more mundane matters of my planet. I find myself very satisfied and content with my daily routine here."

"And will your mother be joining us later for dinner?" I asked in an unassuming manner.

"My mother died a few years ago in a transport accident. Very rare indeed, but they still do occur once or twice a decade."

"Oh, I am sorry, Moori. I did not know. Nor did I mean to pry. It's just that . . . well . . . please forgive me."

"That's quite all right, Robert. As you said previously, it happened a long time ago," she stated in a steady voice as she steered me through the wall. We had entered a room that seemed to be some sort of anteroom. It was a little larger than most anterooms I have found myself waiting in on Earth but, still, much the same as to the interior layout of the room. As I turned and glanced back from where we had entered the chamber, I noticed I now had the ability to see straight through the wall back into the great room we had just exited. I could see Klaatu leaving the room, abruptly disappearing into another section of the house. Moori must have noticed my consternation as she addressed the quizzical look on my face.

"Yes, Robert, every room that adjoins the great room has been designed to have an open view of the great room. This allows us to readily observe anyone who is currently occupying the chamber. This also allows us the distinct ability to prevent any untoward surprises from occurring. However, as you already have observed, no individual occupying the great room can see into any other area of the house. I believe you will find out that most Muuraens highly value their security and privacy."

"Yes, I suppose they do," I answered back in an effort to keep the conversation flowing in a smooth manner. She continued leading me through the anteroom until we, once again, passed magically through a doorway that didn't exist into a room having much more resemblance to an Earth-like master bedroom suite.

At first glance, the immaculate guest suite was sparse in furniture. In fact, I would go so far as to state, it was fairly empty of any fixtures or furnishings. Moori proceeded leisurely across the suite to the opposite wall where existed a row of pulsating lights. The lights were in a rectangular format and were pulsating intermittently. Without bothering to give an explanation, she passed her hand over the whole row of lights then turned back toward me as if to observe my confusion. She seemed to be gazing intently at my face and offered me a warm smile as events began to unfold before me.

From within varying locations throughout the room, solid walls shifted and a fully made bed appeared. Sliding effortlessly and silently out of other walls were a desk and a chair, and a small table with two chairs. From within the floor, several comfortable-looking cushioned chairs slowly elevated into place, along with two nightstand tables, one on either side of the bed. The solid wall of the room bordering the outside environment suddenly turned transparent, allowing me to view the incredible crystalline-pillared scenery of the vast Muuraen landscape. The room was now flooded with light from their blue-white sun. I could also feel a flood of warm but refreshing air flowing into the room and across my body.

Fascinated by the changes, I shifted around nervously and instinctively turned to my right. Unbelievably, I could now observe what can only be described as a master bathroom presenting itself where no room previously existed. I found it quite easy to make out a shower receptacle and a luxuriously long, deep, garden-style tub. A double sink and what only could pass a toilet had also appeared. Another small booth next to the shower area could be seen, but I had no idea what its function could possibly be.

"This will be your suite for as long as you wish to stay with us, Robert," Moori stated in a matter-of-fact tone of voice. "This should be just about all you could require for a comfortable guest room. To operate the controls, just pass your hand over any of the flashing lights located near the facilities. When finished with the fixture of choice, pass your hand over the corresponding light once again. The fixture or furnishing will recede back into its original position."

"What is this booth-type receptacle," I asked as I pointed to the one unknown apparatus in question.

"If you would please step into this fixture after your shower or bath, it will dry you within a couple of seconds, sterilize any germ or bacteria which may be found on your body, and initiate a final cleaning of teeth, fingernails, toenails, and other sections of your body. Once you exit this machine, you will be more clean and free of any bacteria or germ than you have ever been before in your entire existence."

"Not only am I beginning to feel very protected and sheltered," I responded in sincere wonderment of everything I had seen, "but I also am beginning to feel very pampered. You and your father are truly the most generous and kind hosts I have ever met."

"It is not often we have such an honored guest from another galaxy," she replied in a light, feathery voice as she turned, walking gracefully to the opposite side of the room. "Truly, I am the one honored." Moori smiled and made an amiable gesture.

"Please make yourself at home, Robert. Feel free to use our facilities to refresh and relax yourself. I imagine it has been quite a confusing and confounding time for you. I am quite sure you have witnessed and absorbed so many experiences and observations of things and events completely alien to you. I can only imagine what you must be feeling. All of those events have transpired in such a rapid time frame, it truly must be overwhelming. So with your permission, I will withdraw and allow you to attend to your needs. If you desire anything further, please just pass your hand over the top light on the panel, and wherever I am within the residence I will be notified. After you bathe, please avail yourself of our soothing robes located in this small closet. These robes are the traditional attire we wear while at home, and I believe you will find the material very relaxing. Please choose any you like. I will return in a suitable amount of time to pick you up and escort you to dinner."

"Thank you, Moori," I replied. I watched as she finished her slow walk across the length of the guest suite. Moori disappeared through the wall/exit. I was now left alone with my thoughts. Truthfully, I did not feel exhausted, or even a little tired. Some unknown process in the sleep chamber had refreshed me to the point of feeling almost exhilarated. However, the rapidly unwinding sequence of events leading me to these strange surroundings quite overwhelmed me, which had the effect of inducing a mental fatigue. Any immediate analytical pronouncement of prior events was quite beyond me for the moment. But what a wondrous moment!

I sat on the corner of the bed and gazed at the outside environment. It slowly dawned on me that some jagged pinnacles of crystalline rock formations were not in the same place I had seen them minutes before. Due to my mental fatigue, it took some moment for me to realize the house was slowly rotating. I could only imagine that the reason for this was to maximize the effect of the sunlight. The rotation of the dome was a direct effort to ensure the sunlight is evenly distributed throughout each room of the residence. I slowly shook my head in disbelief and amazement.

"This world is endlessly fascinating," I marveled aloud. With supreme effort, I drew my mind from speculation and rose to my feet. I began a slow, deliberate walk toward the master bath, unbuttoning my shirt as I proceeded. I was soon naked in the garden-style tub soaking in a nice hot bath. The water temperature was just right, hot . . . but not scalding. My muscles began to relax and soften under warm influence of the water. It seemed to me there was something a little different about the water on planet Muurae, but I could not recognize what the discernable difference was for the moment. I decided to pass on analyzing the water and just enjoy the bath.

As I shut my eyes, all my thoughts seemed to dissolve as well. I must have soaked for a good thirty minutes. Finally, I arose from the bath and made my way over to the shower. There really was no need to shower other than that I had wanted to try the shower as well. The water pressure was ample, and the water pouring over my face seemed to awake and invigorate me out of the induced tranquility of the bath. I suddenly felt more alive than I had in years. With this thought in my head, I exited the shower and walked over to the receptacle that Moori said would dry and disinfect me. I hesitated in a bit of uncertainty for a moment then stepped in. I waved my hand over the pulsating light. A dry mist of warm air buffeted and soothed my body. The interior of the cubicle suddenly turned deep purple. Within a few seconds, the drying and sanitizing process was promptly finished. I stood outside the cubicle, dried, clean, and refreshed. To my complete surprise, the stubble of my beard had been effectively removed as efficiently as though I had had a close shave. None of my other body hair had been affected. I suppressed a smile as I wondered how they managed to pull that off! As I gazed into a small mirror-type device, I was struck by an extremely intense experience. The image reflecting back was not of a seventy-year-old man but was the smooth, unwrinkled countenance of a thirty-five-year-old. I was dumbstruck. Is it possible to actually reverse the aging process on this planet? And truthfully, I was feeling as though I was thirty-five years old once again. I walked triumphantly through the doorway and back out into the interior of the guest room. As I made my way to the closet to grab a robe, I found myself momentarily stopped at a sole rectangular light embedded in the wall. I gazed at the pulsating light in abstract wonderment.

"Amazing, the technology they have! So advanced from the technology we possessed on planet Earth." I inquisitively passed my hand over the bottom light. "Hmmm, I wonder what this light activates."

A moment later, the voice of Moori came drifting through an unseen speaker system within the guest room. The quality of sound was excellent yet still possessed the quality of being transmitted through a speaker system of some sort.

"Robert?"

"Yes, Moori?"

"You might want to consider passing your hand over the bottom light once again."

"I'm sorry, Moori. Did I do something wrong?"

"No, Robert. At least not exactly, however, by waving your hand over the last light, you activated the reverse transparency equipment of the guest room's structure. As a result, I can clearly see you standing there naked."

Chapter Eleven

Dinner and More

Time: Unknown
Date: Unknown
Location: Planet Muurae

"Robert, may I enter?" the soft musical voice of Moori called from outside the room. For a moment, her voice sounded clear enough to be in the room.

"Certainly," I replied as I stood in the middle of the room in an exquisitely designed robe. The cloth of the robe was unique. Superior to any cloth on Earth. Needless to say, I had never felt anything quite like it. It was warm, soft, and comfortable, and soothed me into quite a relaxed state. Moori entered the room wearing a robe that only served to intensify the beauty she exuded. I felt my eyes widen and my jaw drop in awe as she approached me. I felt I had never before in my life gazed upon such magnificent beauty. She smiled tenderly as she grabbed my arm and began to guide me to the room's exit. I felt a strong desire to allow Moori to lead me wherever she had wanted.

Moori radiated a strong physical influence, along with a kind of innocence, that both captured my imagination and my heart. This feeling of love emerging from deep inside me had not been felt in decades. This feeling was completely unexpected. I had once thought I would never sense such feelings again. Perhaps my libido had been renewed and refreshed with the rest of my body!

"For dinner, we are having one of your favorite meals, Robert. I believe spaghetti with meat sauce, a nice green salad, along with some wonderfully toasted garlic bread is among your favorite meals?"

"Indeed! But how did you know?"

"Father remembered from the time he spent with you many years ago. He said you had quite an appetite as a young boy! We are hoping the size of your appetite has not changed."

"Moori, I feel as hungry as I did when I was a boy!" I responded with a smile. "My appetite seems to have returned, and even grown a little."

"Excellent, Robert! The salad will made of a mixture of Muurae vegetables and Earth's vegetables. Father had picked up some seeds while visiting your planet and has cultivated them on Muurae. The meat in the tomato sauce will be a synthetic blend from our replicators, but I am willing to bet you will not be able to tell the difference," she stated with a wink.

Moori was projecting a vibrance that was almost overwhelming. Her smile and enthusiasm promptly assured me, working to diffuse any uneasy feeling about the dinner I may have secretly harbored. I actually found myself eagerly anticipating the sampling of some of their local dishes. Perhaps it was at this time the seed began to germinate within my mind about the possibilities of staying on planet Muurae in a more permanent status . . . a resident alien? My second impression of life on this planet had already began forming in my mind. There could be real happiness to find here. Something I had not felt for many years was stirring deep within me.

"Moori . . ." I said, pausing to take a moment to fully realize the import of what I was about to say, "I am afraid there has been quite an unexpected development . . ."

"I suppose that is only to be expected," she replied before I could finish my statement. "After all, you have just been through an extremely intense experience."

"No, I mean . . . I find myself on the planet with the most advanced race in the galaxy, and I am fascinated by every aspect, everything I have experienced, seen, touched . . ."

"Robert, I can imagine there are many overwhelming sensations . . ."

"No, Moori, it is more than that . . . I . . . want to say . . ."

The conversation ended abruptly and perhaps a bit awkwardly as she escorted me into the dining area where Klaatu was already standing next to a lavishly set table. I had to force myself back into a more proper mind-set, wanting to, at the very least, observe minimum protocol suitable for the occasion. Klaatu swiftly approached me, holding an ornately manufactured glass in his outstretched hand. The etchings upon the glass were of a type I had never seen before. They were remarkable in their beauty.

"Robert, come and join me in sampling some of our finer Muuraean wine. I think you will find the flavor and bouquet somewhat extraordinary," he said with a warm and welcoming smile, which emphasized and underscored his friendship that he evidently felt toward me. It had been many years since I had any friends to speak of, and I could not imagine a better friend to have on any world than Klaatu. This was a man of absolute integrity and principle.

"Father is very proud of his wine. A mixture of Earth and Muuraean grapes," stated Moori with a beautiful smile on her face.

"I would be delighted, sir," I replied with the utmost respect. A relieved realization suddenly struck me that the dinner seemed to be proceeding along the more familiar line instead of the formal line. This had an immediate effect of putting me at ease, in a more relaxed frame of mind. I was among good friends here and could calm my nerves.

As I gingerly accepted the glass of wine from his hand, he reached down and grabbed another glass and handed it to Moori.

"I propose a toast," Klaatu continued as he raised his glass slightly. "To Dr. Robert Benson, whom I affectionately call Bobby . . . we are truly delighted and honored by your visit, and hope you will consider our rather humble abode to be your home. May you find all the happiness you seek while staying with us. And may your time here be of the utmost enlightenment and enjoyment."

I took a quick sip of the proffered wine. It tasted strong and sweet, and had no aftertaste attached to it at all. It went down very smooth. I let the taste linger upon my palate for a moment, savoring every drop. Feeling the mood, I felt a strong urge to return a toast.

"I, also, propose a toast. To my longtime friend, Klaatu, and his most lovely daughter, Moori. I could never hope, no matter how many planets or stars I visit in my lifetime, to meet a better class of individuals that I could have the distinct honor and privilege of being able to call . . . my friends. God bless you both."

We all raised our glasses in unison, enjoying another sip of the Muuraen wine. The wine seemed to grow sweeter with each sip and also began to exhibit an almost imperceptible fruity flavor. I was instantly reminded of a sangria. And yet, there was a much more alluring taste to this wine. I immediately thought, "I could get used to this." The dinner seemed to be off to a good start. I was genuinely looking forward to the camaraderie and the conversation, as well as the food. The spaghetti sauce looked fabulous, and I could actually notice the aromatic smell of garlic emanating from the bread. Klaatu observed my quick glance at the food and waved me amicably to my seat.

"Please be seated, Robert," he said in a relaxed, congenial tone of voice. The aromatic allure of the cuisine beckoned me, and for the first time since I had arrived on this planet, I felt a growing sense of hunger. As I sat down at the large circular dinner table, a huge portion of spaghetti with meat sauce was placed upon my plate by Moori. She also served her father then herself.

"Klaatu," I said after sampling my first bite of Muuraean spaghetti, which rivaled that of any I had sampled on Earth, "this is extremely good spaghetti!"

"I'm glad you are enjoying it," he laughed heartily. "This is my own special recipe. As a matter of fact, you are the first foreigner to taste my spaghetti, so I was secretly hoping you would enjoy it. I know you are a spaghetti expert, so I am extremely happy you approve."

"So do you always do your own cooking then," I asked as I stuffed another forkful into my mouth. The flavoring of the sauce was sweet, but not overpowering.

"Yes, we do, at least for much of the time. Quite infrequently, we are required to attend a function that provides sustenance, but both Moori and I like to cook. It is kind of a pride and passion of ours. We grow most of our own food in the solarium, which, by the way, I would be happy to give you a tour of later. Knowing your sharp powers of observation, I believe you may find a few points of absorbing interest in our solarium. Anyway, we know what we like to consume, and we cook it to our precise specifications."

"Yes, thank you. I would embrace the opportunity to study your solarium! I cherish the opportunity to learn as much as I can about your home, your planet, the galaxy, your society . . . everything. I am beginning to feel as excited as a child in a new candy shop. So many new things to see, do, taste. I want to experience as much as possible. There is so much fantastic technology here. I must say, Klaatu, you Muuraens have really built something special among the stars. In bleak contrast, I am afraid the people of Earth must seem hopelessly primitive to you."

Klaatu smiled briefly at the compliment then took another sip from his wineglass. My initial sense of isolation and estrangement from the Earth had completely vanished, being replaced by a warm and welcome feeling. Good friends, good food, and good wine is a magical recipe! After I took a prolonged sip from my wineglass, I continued the conversation.

"I have observed that the material used in the construction of your residence seems to be of the same type and quality as is used in your spaceships."

"Yes, very good, Robert. It is exactly the same," replied Klaatu as he pushed the salad bowl toward me. "Try some more of our homegrown salad. I think you'll find the salad and the dressing more than satisfactory to your taste."

The salad actually seemed to become more savory and delicious with each bite. The garlic bread was possessed of a zesty garlic flavor but was not overpowering in taste. But the salad and the bread were quite delicious. As I stuffed another forkful of spaghetti into my mouth, Klaatu continued.

"Our planet is largely water, with two massive continents separating the oceans. Both continents are about equally populated, with the continent opposite ours being the more industrialized side. The continent we are on is a bit more concerned with agricultural activities. Nearly everyone on our planet is engaged in activities that in some way or another benefits the inhabitants of our planet and the other planets of the Association. Our Association of

Planets is comprised of two planets in our solar system and three in the closest neighboring solar system, located on the opposite side of our sun. The neighboring solar system has two stars and ten planets, three of which are inhabitable. The other beings in our galaxy are very similar to us, however, there are a couple of species existing which bear no resemblance to the unique human form. We have a working relationship with all species. Some, however, are more sociable than others."

"Fascinating! While I am extremely intrigued by other alien life-forms within your galaxy, I am, first and foremost greatly interested in the society that has evolved here on Muurae," I stated with a rising tone of interest and excitement in my voice. "There seems to be such technological triumphs! The things I have so far observed on your planet are decades away from anything we could accomplish on Earth."

"I find your enthusiasm most refreshing, Robert," said Klaatu with a broad smile crossing his face. He leaned forward, his face wrinkled in thought, and stared intently into my eyes. If the effect was to emphasize and underscore his next point, he was eminently successful.

"I think you could find yourself in agreement with the Association of Planets on how productive a peaceful society can become when there is no credible threat of war. Technological innovation occurs at a much more rapid pace in a peaceful society than within a society that is constantly dealing with the imminent threat of war. We have essentially been able to pool all of our collective efforts into accomplishing wonderful technological achievements to the benefit of all, rather than wasting a lot of time, talent, and effort on pursuing inherently evil interests."

"That has been a point well-taken with me for quite some time. I wish the governments of Earth would have spent more time and money in such pursuits, instead of pursuing their warlike ideologies. We have had to pay too heavy of a price. Which brings up the interesting point of currency in your world. What does your Association of Planets use for money? Is it all one currency, or does every planet in the association have their own form of currency?"

"The primary currency used with the Association of Planets is . . . diamonds . . . I believe you call them," answered Moori as her father had just placed a forkful of spaghetti into his mouth. I turned my attention to her as she continued her explanation. "We do, also, have some minor forms such as gold, silver, and cantrite, all in the form of bars and coins. Silver and cantrite are used among the peoples of our planet, while transactions between planets are solely reserved to the providence of diamonds. However, on Muurae, most of our day-to-day transactions usually include the form of . . . bartering. Is that the right term, Robert?"

"If you mean exchanging goods for services instead of utilizing any form of currency, then yes, you are absolutely correct in your semantics," I replied as I gave a short, dry laugh. "You really have a sound grasp of our language, Moori."

"Father has been instructing me in the hopes that one day in the future, I would have the opportunity to use my knowledge," she said mildly. "Of course, I was hoping to be able to use it as well. I guess I did not have as much faith as my father the day would actually arrive. However, studying extraterrestrial languages is a hobby of mind, I suppose. Since Father's visit to your planet, I have especially been fascinated by your society and its struggles. I clearly remember the stories he used to tell me about his space travels when I was a child. Your country, the United States of America, for example, Robert, started off in such a hopeful fashion. The founders of your country put forth such noble ideas . . ."

"Which we as people destroyed in such a short time?" I stated wistfully as I broke off a piece of garlic bread and stuffed it in my mouth.

"Yes," stated Moori in a steady voice. "I am puzzled as to how this could happen."

"Well, Moori, my theory is . . . Americans grew fat, lazy, and apathetic to what their elected members of government were doing. As this transpired, our government grew stronger, and conversely the power of the people grew weaker. Once you give away any right, chances are you will not get those rights back. The government no longer feared the people, but people began fearing the government. Then the government, solidly in control of what once was the people's power, and with no real opposition from the people to challenge their evildoing, politicians acted very swiftly to consolidate their power. To do this, they needed more money from the people, so they created taxes then swiftly raised taxes. Then they created enforcement agencies to forcefully take money from the people. This terrorist agency was called the Internal Revenue Service. This agency enacted terrible penalties against anyone protesting taxation. People had their lands, homes, bank accounts . . . confiscated. It didn't matter if you were sick, unemployed, struggling . . . they attacked everyone the same. Except . . . for their own members of government, that is.

These legislators the people had elected had special exemptions from the laws others had to obey. Many of these legislators often became legislators for life! They then voted themselves pay raises while the people they were supposedly representing were losing money and starving! They voted themselves pensions for life, even if they served only four or six years! And the people still did nothing! The government then aligned itself with huge, rich corporations, which would then lavish the congressmen and senators with money and gifts! Soon, only the rich could afford to campaign and run for office. Once elected, the senators and congressmen enriched themselves via graft and corruption until they became even more powerful. And still the American people did nothing! These self-anointed legislators effectively raped the American people and laughed! They told them, "Don't complain, the rape is good for you! We know what is good for you!" And . . . the American people did nothing. As long as the American people had beer to drink and television to watch at night, they were happy. They did not care about the freedoms and rights their government stole from them. Then, it was too late."

"I am sorry, Robert," Moori responded genuinely as she sipped on her glass of wine. She seemed to be momentarily lost in thought over what I had just said. I decided to remain quiet for a few minutes to compose myself. Eventually, I turned my attention back toward Klaatu. It was evident he had been listening intently to what I said. He seemed deeply distressed and saddened by my analysis of American history as I saw it.

"Tell me, Klaatu," I said as I picked up my glass of wine, holding it in front of me,. "what about your form of government? I am interested in how your race of people have successfully developed a more efficient and representative form of government, which I must say, seems to be impervious to corruption. I can only imagine what that is like."

"Well, Bobby, I can assure you it is completely opposite of the evolution of your government, I am happy to say," replied Klaatu with a sly, disarming smile. "We of Muurae, much like your original Founding Fathers, believe in the least form of government as possible. In fact, the roles of legislators, representatives, and lawyers are very low-level types of occupations. It has been our experience a society can exist with just a few laws, somewhat akin to your Ten Commandments. Therefore, any law which is brought up for consideration, must be passed by at least 75 percent of the population of the planet. Therefore, no unpopular or unjust law could possibly be passed into existence. Consequently, there are no unpopular laws passed on to an unwilling public like there is in your society.

"The very thought of government is abhorrent to our way of life. Since we have very few legislators, and they serve only part time, they do not feel compelled to necessarily enact any form of legislation. There can be no power grabs by any set of individuals or groups of individuals. There is no one group that is more important than another. As a result, we have no taxes, no taking by our government of anything they did not earn on their own accord. Governments, for the most part, earn nothing in and of themselves. Our form of government has no power to enact any law on their own. There, however, was a time in our planet's history where a group of individuals tried to usurp power from the people they served. They were dealt with rather harshly . . . tried as traitors. No one has attempted such an act since."

"I see," I responded as I took another sip of wine.

"For our mutual protection, the Association of Planets have a fleet of twenty-five spaceships capable of intergalactic travel. Aboard each ship is a robot . . . Gort. Each robot is an exact duplicate of the other. All have the same programming and functions. Sometimes, special emissaries like myself, accompany them on their intergalactic journey. However, if their mission is merely one of enforcement, then they travel alone. Once the terrible and extremely difficult decision has been made to enforce a destructive policy on a particular planet, then no emissary is allowed to accompany the robot on its mission. This has the desired effect of preventing any emotion from interfering with the execution of a robot's mission. Once the spaceship leaves our planet, no being is permitted to influence the outcome of the mission."

"So that is why Gort traveled to Earth by itself . . ." I said as my thoughts trailed off. The result of Gort's visits were still too fresh and horrible to contemplate.

"Exactly. I am sorry about what has happened to your planet, Robert. The governments of Earth were warned not to bring their destructive powers out into space. They foolishly failed to heed those warnings. I do not understand why."

"Because the governments of Earth were populated by people with arrogant minds," I replied coldly as I took a deep breath in an effort to remain calm.

"Yes, and unfortunately, that arrogance has cost them a huge price in the lives of the people they were duly elected to represent," he said scathingly. It was readily apparent Klaatu was still possessed of anger regarding the unfortunate situation.

"Please believe me, Robert, when I say . . . it was my sincere hope the governments populating your Earth would have heeded the warning of our Association of Planets. I apologize to you I was not more successful in my mission to Earth. As for the members of the Association of Planets, it remains a point of pride with us that we have not allowed small-minded, selfish individuals the power to make decisions for the rest of us. I am sure the founders of the United States of America never envisioned the depths of depravity to which your country would eventually sink."

"On the contrary, Klaatu, men like Thomas Jefferson did envision what may happen in the future of our growing government. Jefferson warned of the methods our government officials could employ to corrupt our country. However, it was always the wish of the American people that our government officials would overcome their arrogance and power-hungry attitudes. Sadly, this was my mother's wish as well as my own. It was, unfortunately, a wish unfulfilled . . ." I said in a subdued and mournful voice.

"Your mother was a brave and intelligent woman. She was always honest and sincere in her interactions with me. I do miss her, Robert." Klaatu's eyes were sullen.

"So do I," I stated simply as I stared down at my spaghetti. Myriad gentle thoughts and memories of my mother flowed sweetly, yet sorrowfully through my mind. In the space of the moment, I failed to notice the somber silence that now pervaded the atmosphere at the table. Once I realized what transpired, I thought it now incumbent upon me to lighten the mood.

"Say, what's going on here? Is this a funeral, a wake? Klaatu, enough of the bleak and somber topics. Tell me about what has transpired in your life since you returned from Earth those many years ago."

A smile summarily lit up his face. I glanced momentarily at Moori, and she was smiling too. The sour and somber mood had lifted as suddenly as it had come.

"The universe has been nothing but kind to us since my return. We have prospered greatly and are living the life we desire. I spend most of my time working in my garden and laboratory. However, I am sometimes called upon for consultation by the Association of Planets in some important matter or another. Sometimes it even proves to be a healthy distraction from my everyday routines. The council for the Association of Planets has sent me to several other planets, in and out of our galaxy, as an emissary. On a couple of occasions, I was honored to make first contact with two planets, which had evidenced their readiness and ability for our official invitation to join the Association of Planets. All in all, Robert, I'd say I have been happily busy. The only unfortunate event, which has befallen me in my life has been the untimely and tragic death of my wife, Koori. That event happened before I visited your civilization, Robert. Since her death, I had slowed my work for the Association and concentrated on spending time with Moori. That was a decision I have never regretted."

Klaatu smiled a warm and charming smile as he shifted his glance toward his lovely daughter. Moori reached over and delicately patted her father's hand.

"Well, Klaatu, I truly must say I find your side of the galaxy very interesting. From the moment of my awakening from the induced sleep aboard the spaceship, I have felt about as well as I have in the last thirty years. I have noticed I not only feel younger, I look younger," I stated as I popped another forkful of salad into my mouth.

"While you were sleeping, it seems our medical technology system aboard the ship diagnosed several problems within your body," stated Klaatu calmly. "The biological infestations were sterilized . . . eliminated as a routine course of action. The aging process within your body has been dramatically reduced to almost negligible factor. All the biological systems of your body have been effectively cleaned and repaired by the process. I conservatively estimate your body should feel like it did when you were age thirty-five. Here, on the planet Muurae, every time we dry ourselves after bathing, the process of purification is repeated. I am 131 years old, but I feel much younger."

"No side effects from the unfortunate gunshot wound you suffered on Earth so many years ago?" I asked with a sense of incredulity rising in my voice.

"Oh, there has been some, to be sure. One cannot completely escape the effects of the injury. After all, a traumatic wound is still a traumatic wound anywhere in the universe," he responded mildly, without much sense of concern in his voice. "I could scarcely expect there to be no residual harm to my body, but I have lived a full and happy life. I certainly have nothing to complain about. And you, Robert? An astrophysicist and quantum mechanics physicist, professor, and lecturer? It would seem you have lived a full life as well since I departed the earth."

"Yes, Klaatu. I owe most of my comparatively simple accomplishments in life to you. You see, it was your visit to our planet and your stay with our family, which effectively spurred on my interest in these fields of study. Ever since you left our planet over half a century ago, I wanted to contribute to our people being able, someday in the not too distant future, to be able to do what your people had done. Accomplish what your people have accomplished. I had hoped we, as a civilization, would benefit from your visit. Now, our people will never get the chance to profit from your knowledge and friendship."

"I would not be so sure, Robert," said Klaatu as he put down his fork and leaned toward me. He stared intently at me as his eyes narrowed, his thin lips momentarily compressed. "A similar opportunity may occur. This brings up an important subject I wish to discuss with you."

I immediately put down my fork and returned his steady gaze with one of my own. The sudden seriousness from Klaatu riveted my attention, and I somehow thought an unexpected development was altogether likely to be presented to me. This could be a penultimate moment in my life. I waited patiently and listened thoughtfully as he spoke.

"We, of the Association of Planets, have been aware of your pending arrival since the moment of its inception. We had transmitted orders to Gort to safeguard your arrival to Muurae at all costs. I assure you, Robert, all measures deemed necessary to ensure your safety were implemented. In the weeks before your arrival, there had been a constant flurry of activity within the sacred chambers of the council. All concerned with the resultant part you could play in the future sequence of events . . ."

"Part?" I asked in a stunned and quizzical voice. The word quivered in my brain.

"Yes," continued Klaatu as his eyes widened slightly then narrowed once again. "The council believes you can play an extremely significant role in the future of your planet. I would hazard to say you will be of the utmost importance to the future well-being of your planet. Perhaps, the most important man in the history of your world."

"But . . . but how? I don't see . . ."

"The insight, intelligence, and courage you displayed in the face of adversity, along with your strong diplomatic skills, will make you the ideal choice to return to Earth as an emissary representing the Supreme Council and the Association of Planets."

"What!" I exclaimed in openmouthed astonishment. I immediately felt the immensity of the words just spoken . . . my confusion was readily apparent. I felt myself shift uneasily in my seat . . . nervously awaiting the next few sentences to come.

"Yes, Robert," replied Klaatu in a deadly earnest tone of voice, "the council wishes you to return to Earth and represent our best wishes, along with our greatest hope for establishing the correct philosophy and attitude among the peoples of Earth. It is our sincere wish that your planet would, in the not too distant future, join us. The Association of Planets is constantly striving to engage and befriend peaceful planets with the intent of bringing them into our rather small but growing confederation of planets and civilizations. The benefit to the peoples of Earth would be monumental. All of our advancements in science and technology would be theirs. Your people would have the knowledge and capacity to turn deserts into thriving farmlands, to eliminate all sickness and disease from their peoples, allowing for the first time in your recorded history, the ability to focus all your people's considerable energies and talents into peaceful pursuits. We would welcome them into the Association of Planets, inviting them to join us in exploring unknown universes and galaxies together."

"Return to Earth?' I stammered, the shock of his statements initiating a broiling chaos of thoughts in my mind. I shuddered under the continuing impact of his carefully chosen words. "But . . . but I just got here . . ."

"I know this comes as a bit of a shock, Robert," Klaatu responded, his voice sounding firm and reassuring, "but I assure you, the Supreme Council's thinking on this matter of extreme importance was not haphazard or extemporaneous. An irreplaceable amount of effort by members of the council has been expended to even seriously consider putting this proposition to you. I hope you don't mind, Robert, but I'm afraid it was my idea. The Supreme Council was unsure of my idea when it was first stated, but I assured the members that placing the utmost confidence in your abilities to successfully complete this assignment . . . would not be a mistake. I'm afraid I am the one who has put you on the hot seat, Bobby."

I began to recover a portion of my senses as I frantically raced to absorb what had been proposed. I slowly put down my fork, allowing me a precious few seconds to think. As soon as I could breathe comfortably again, I spoke, "Klaatu, I sincerely appreciate the confidence you have placed in me, but I was hoping to stay on your planet . . . study the wonders of your civilization, your society, your universe. There is so much to learn . . ."

Klaatu abruptly cut me off with a wave of his hand, gesturing significantly. His brown eyes glinted and winked, as his face broke into a strange smile.

"And so you shall, if that is your wish. I personally welcome you with all my heart, Robert. You will always be welcomed in our home. However, I must ask of you one more task before you settle down into a life of wonder on our planet. Without this mission to Earth, it is greatly feared among the council members that the destruction of your home planet must inevitably reoccur. Without our direction and guidance, it is likely the people of Earth will revert to their old ways. Robert, your trip will be short and sweet, as you Earthlings are fond of saying. I promise you, your return to Earth will be no more than a year at most. Perhaps, possibly a great deal shorter. The calculated time for the duration of your mission will necessarily depend upon how the people of Earth accept our efforts to recognize, reeducate, and guide them in an acceptable direction. As you Earthmen are also fond of saying, the time is ripe for change. After what has transpired on Earth, we conjecture the people will be afraid . . . suspicious of our offer to extend our hand in friendship. They will be very wary of our help."

"You think!" I asked facetiously, trying desperately to grasp the difficult concept being presented.

"Considering the fact the Association of Planets just executed three-fourths of the population of Earth, I guess they would have good reason to be suspicious of your proffered generosity and kindness. How the hell do you expect me to overcome—"

"As only a fellow Earthman can do. I am sure we would encounter some resistance in our efforts, perhaps even fierce resistance," interrupted Klaatu. "However, a person of their own planet, of their own race, a person known and trusted—"

"That's just the thing," I exclaimed, as I interrupted Klaatu, offering up an explanation of sorts, "I was not well known on our planet. I was not in politics. I was not a star athlete, or even a celebrity of any sort. In fact, very few people knew me. This mission could be tantamount to suicide for me!"

"Yes," replied Klaatu with an amiable gesture. He slowly picked up his half-full wineglass and held it momentarily in front of his lips. "We have considered that fact. We believe this point may well work in your favor. If you had been in politics, no one would believe you, anyway. You would have been marked as a liar and deceiver. People are smart enough to know the politicians and government officials of Earth are liars, cheaters, and thieves. They would rightly blame anyone in politics as being responsible for the tragic events recently experienced on Earth. As for celebrities . . . their opinions are useless, as are the star athlete's opinions. Most people of Earth realize celebrities and athletes are there to entertain. But you, Robert, a scientist, a visitor to our planet . . . an alien civilization, the man who has seen, accomplished, and traveled throughout space more than any other Earthman would be a highly credible source of information. I should think . . . no . . . I am certain of my unshakable belief, that if we are to save the Earth and its people, you are the one man for the task. You are the only man for the task!"

I slumped back unsteadily in my chair. The enormous complexity of what was now being asked of me was more than the normal laws of perspective could conceive. An unimaginable cacophony of sounds, thoughts, and images coursed through my mind. Everything seemed doubly unreal to me. I slowly glanced up toward Moori, and she smiled sweetly, returning my gaze momentarily. The reasoning ability of my mind seemed to be lost beyond all recall. I smiled at the absurdity of the thought, the mission, I was being asked to perform. I suddenly felt terribly alone beneath an alien sky.

As I glanced upward toward the peak of the dome structure, I noticed a shining of spectral, lunar light . . . a dazzling silver crescent. The crystal dome windows glittered in their magnificence. My dreams of a life upon planet Muurae began melting in the mounting frustration consuming my mind. What was becoming abundantly clear was a realization I really did not seem to have much choice in the matter. The atmosphere in the room had abruptly become hushed and expectant. Klaatu, sensing my reluctance and confusion, finally, almost hesitantly, spoke in a small effort to reassure me.

"Robert, the Supreme Council of the Association of Planets, of course, will not force you to go. You may stay here with us without any fear of offense or dishonor. The council fully realizes the magnitude of the request presented to you."

"Thank you, Klaatu, for those comforting words," I replied in a low, calm voice as I sat up straight in my chair. The sudden sense of foreboding that had rapidly swept over me seemed to now slowly depart as quickly as it came. I had regained my senses and composure enough to respond in a more intelligent manner. Gathering my thoughts, I closed my eyes and spoke, "I guess I could not, in all clear conscience, carefully and sensibly reject the task which has been presented to me. I am quite sure you are sincere when you state I would not be held up to ridicule and scorn on your planet, by your people, if I refused this request. Moreover, however, I could not live with myself as a man if I did not accept this critical mission to save the Earth from further destruction. I would most assuredly scorn and ridicule myself for the refusal, and that to me would be a worse punishment than being ridiculed and scorned by others. Therefore, I wholeheartedly accept the Supreme Council's recommendation. I will do as I am tasked by the council. Klaatu, you have my express permission to inform the Supreme Council of my acceptance of this mission to Earth."

"Splendid, Robert!" Klaatu chortled triumphantly with a widening smile. He made no nominal effort to cover the mixture of relief and joy in his voice.

As I shifted my gaze toward Moori, I could not help but note a look of bewilderment in her eyes. My announcement seemed to have stirred her unexpectedly. I forced a tired smile at her and slowly returned my attention to finishing off the rest of my meal. My own heartbeat seemed to be drowning out any other sound in the room. There was no sense in putting up any unsuccessful pretense of being anything but sad on the upcoming departure from Muurae. A sole tear formed in my eye. Moori must have seen it.

"Do not be sad, Robert. You are doing a quite wonderful thing. I do not believe most Earthmen would agree to do what you have agreed to do. I am most proud of you."

"Thank you, Moori," I replied as I dabbed the tear away, trying to do so without any obvious effort. I observed her eyes were now frantically bright.

"I truly am humbled and honored I have been asked to do this. Quite overwhelmed, really. It is just everything seems to be happening at the speed of light right now. The incredible speed of events and the concurrent adjustments required . . . produce the effect of overwhelming the senses. That's all."

"Robert," the voice of Klaatu seemed to have a much softer tone, which matched the softer look on his face, "It is we who are honored. I give you my word, you will have a lifetime to accomplish all you wish to do on Muurae, and in this galaxy upon your return. However, I feel I must warn you . . . once you return to Earth and are among your own people once again, your wish to return may slowly disappear altogether. It is altogether possible, logical, you may want to stay on Earth. It is not so easy for anyone to leave their home planet and exist on another planet, living happily ever after."

"No, Klaatu, there is really nothing left on earth for me to cling to at all. Everyone and everything I knew and loved are all gone," I replied with sober objectivity. I finished the last forkful of spaghetti and dabbed my garlic bread in the remainder of the rich sauce. Grabbing the goblet of wine, I gulped down the last bit of wine, and held out the glass in front of me.

"May I be permitted another glass of this rather excellent Muraean wine?"

I awoke with a start from a drowsy, half-conscious condition, slowly rubbing the sleep from my eyes. A warm dawn filled the room. Taking a moment to acclimate myself to the situation, I stood up groggily, then unsteadily, and with a modicum of effort, made my way toward the shower. The warm water splashing softly against my face worked wonders in an effort to rid myself of the minor lethargy I was feeling. It was only a matter of moments before I became refreshed and totally awake. After what seemed like hours under the caressing flow of water, I took a hesitant step forward and eased myself out of the shower. The shower's automatic sensor system noted my leaving and turned the water off. Stepping into the drying and sanitizing chamber, the flow of warm, soothing air drying my body finished the job of reviving me to a fully relaxed and aware state. I felt almost human, again.

I smiled sheepishly at the thought of being human, especially on an alien planet! A sudden sense of calm expectation began to flow through me. Today, at long last, was the day I was scheduled to return to the Earth in my newly appointed capacity as an emissary of the Associations of Planets. I had been informed the trip would take only about thirty days—Earth time—and I would be in a deep and dreamless state of hibernation while aboard the spacecraft. For a fleeting instant I thought about bolting . . . but to where? I shook the irrational thought from my mind as I stepped out from the drying and sanitizing cubicle. What I was about to do seemed to be beyond all reason. But with scarcely a second thought, I began to dress, donning the specially designed spacesuit that had been delivered to me last night. As I effortlessly slipped it on and zipped up the front of the suit, I could not help but think about what was to come. The suit fit as snuggly as possible without being uncomfortable.

"I'm going to be a helluva sight," I thought ruefully.

For many days I had wondered how my return to Earth would be accepted. Perhaps the people of earth would think me a traitor, representing the race of beings who were responsible for the destruction of most of the Earth. For some reason, I could not consider any reaction from the people of Earth except out-and-out rejection. Old memories of Earth were stirring nervously within me. I found myself involuntarily looking up at the transparent dome ceiling of the residence as if I could possibly espy the Earth or its moon. I could only imagine the luminous whirlpools of the galaxy swirling and spinning away from me as my spaceship sped through space at an incredible speed. Moons, stars, and nebulae—all would recede and fall away as I passed from one galaxy to another. My spaceship would sweep past frozen planets and superhot suns. I could imagine an alternating scene of whirling, circular patterns of darkness in space followed inexorably by the dazzling brilliance and explosion of light from nearby suns as I sped through space. It would all be a glimpse of something very strange and wonderful, something to delight all my senses. I had presented the argument for ultimately staying conscious throughout the flight and hoped it was accepted. I would find out shortly. It was easy for me to suppose how I would be half hypnotized and half astonished by what I could possibly experience in this star trek. I was conscious of a rising tension and anxiety within me, but worked hard and efficiently to quiet the fear. I was abruptly startled out of my reverie.

"Good morning, Robert," the voice of Klaatu came out of nowhere. I had not yet gotten used to this ability to communicate with anyone, anywhere, and at anytime in the house as a matter of routine. "How does the suit fit?"

"I'm as snug as a bug in a rug," I answered, as I smiled to no one in particular.

"Excuse me?"

"An old Earth saying," I said as I slipped on the accompanying gloves. "The suit fits fine."

"Excellent. Any second thoughts about doing this?"

"Only about a hundred million," I said with a short laugh. "Let's get this show on the road before I change my mind. Where's Moori?"

"She had to go out for a while this morning. She said she might be able to meet us at the spaceship," replied Klaatu in a matter-of-fact tone of voice.

"I hope so," I sighed with a troubled voice. "I had wanted to say good-bye to her in person. I have become very fond of Moori in the short amount of time I have been here."

"Yes, well, I am sorry, but sometimes duty calls," he replied crisply, and without much sympathy. "Ready to go?"

"I am all yours."

The ride to the nearest spaceport containing the selected ship I was scheduled to travel in was perhaps only ten minutes distance from the residence. The ride over in the bug-car was feeling a bit awkward. My attention was split between what I was supposed to be concentrating on in regard to my mission and wistful thoughts of Moori. I forced myself to concentrate wholly upon the list of instructions, directions, and orders concerning my emissary mission. But once again, my thoughts were frequently distracted by the beautiful image of Moori. There could be no doubt I was greatly disappointed she was not around to see me off on my great adventure. I missed her presence greatly, perhaps even more than I would have cared to admit. I had always held my feelings toward others very close to my chest. At times it had cost me; at other times it had saved me. Now, however, I found it very hard to conceal how I felt about Moori. On the other hand, I had no idea how she felt about me. "Damn, I hate this . . ." I thought to myself. "Why does being human have to be so hard?"

The bug-car came to an abrupt halt. As usual, there was no hidden jolt or shock to the stop. As always, everything running on Muurae did so smoothly. Klaatu and I alighted from the vehicle and walked toward the extended walkway of the spaceship. Gort was standing motionless on the ship, next to the walkway. I involuntarily stopped a moment. A short chill ran through my body every time I found myself in proximity to the robot.

"Come on," stated Klaatu easily, "I will accompany you aboard for your preflight routine."

I managed a quick look around the immediate area, straining to catch some glimpse of Moori, but there was none. I felt my heart sink into a state of despondency and despair. Klaatu remained silent as we made our way up the pathway toward the interior of the ship. My head was tilted dejectedly downward as I watched myself step slowly up the path. As we reached the point of entry I stopped and, again, gave one last look around, trying desperately to catch that longed-for glimpse of Moori. I strained my sight but to no avail. There was no Moori. I sighed dejectedly. It was obvious to me she would not appear to say good-bye. I was in the act of turning my attention toward the interior of the spacecraft when I heard a sugary voice shout out.

"What are you waiting for, Robert? We have a trip to make!"

The voice belonged to Moori! She had already assumed her station inside the spaceship and was wearing the same type of space suit as I was wearing. I was stunned speechless. She reached out and pulled me close to her, kissing me passionately.

"What?" she exclaimed in a light, cheery voice after the duration of the kiss. "You don't think I am about to let the man I love go traipsing and gallivanting all across the universe by himself, do you?"

Epilogue

"I am about to leave the planet Earth for the last time," I stated in a clear and distinct voice. I knew I was not only addressing the crowd that assembled in front of the spaceship but also every single individual on the planet. My voice was automatically being translated into every different language on the planet, and transmitted or broadcasted simultaneously to every nation as well. Everyone on Earth now had the very same capability to do this, as the council elders had given the universal translating technology to the people of this planet. If used in the method specified by the Grand Council of the Association of Planets, there should be no more miscommunication between the peoples of Earth. Communication will now be much more manageable, and it was reasoned this, in an of itself, should be a sufficient start to reducing the mistrust existing among the peoples of the Earth. I continued my departing remarks.

"I have been back on the Earth for a period of 322 days. At the inevitable conclusion of my stay, I have found myself especially proud of the new start toward a better and more profitable life demonstrated by all the peoples of Earth. The initiative and energy put forth has been truly inspirational. Under the governance, authority, and direction of Chief Administrator Jack Holloway, the new United Continents of Earth have progressed enormously toward the goal of becoming a peaceful and prosperous planet. With the updated technology provided by the Association of Planets, we have repaired and/or constructed new buildings, new homes, new factories, and farms. Poverty has ceased, war has disappeared, and famine is no longer an issue. Countries and landscapes once scorched to the bone have been reinvigorated. Farms and farmlands worldwide are now growing plentiful crops. These bountiful yields feed the populace of the world. With technological innovations generously presented to Earth by the Association of Planets, we will soon triple the amount of food produced on this planet. Our new technology has allowed us to irrigate deserts, effectively turning the once-desolate sand dunes into thriving farmlands. Due to the introduction of these new technologies, an unmistakable metamorphosis has begun to transform our planet. All of Earth's people, for the first time in the history of the Earth, now live free from fear or trepidation. Governmental tyranny has been abolished. The people of this planet are now united and working for the good of Earth. No longer will evil be allowed or tolerated by any country or any nation on Earth."

I found myself stopping momentarily as wild applause, shouting, and joyful cries roared out simultaneously from every part of the assembled crowd. Incredibly, there were no looks of stony impassivity. In my wildest dreams, I never imagined this moment in time would have ever occurred. As with most human beings, nagging doubts always seemed to plague me. I smiled and waved then motioned for the crowd to quiet. Once a quiet order was restored, I continued with my speech.

"My friends . . . my countrymen, there is still much work to be done. However, with the guidance provided by the Association of Planets and with the pledge and promise of even newer, more sophisticated technology to help bring about the rapid advance of this new and improved culture of Earth, I believe it will be only a short time before the Association of Planets will offer the great people of Earth the singular opportunity to join them in all their peaceful pursuits. I pledge to you . . . I will personally submit your request, as a peaceful planet, for inclusion into this wonderful association. I am sure they will welcome the people of Earth with open arms and receptive hearts."

Once again, appreciative applause broke out and made the rounds through the assembled crowd. My heart swelled with pride as I observed the smiling, eager faces of the people. The crowd seemed alert to every word, every gesture. I could sense this was the decisive and critical juncture in Earth's history. I exhaled a deep breath and continued.

"As for now, I have been able to produce, with the help of my beautiful wife Moori, a full trade agreement with the Supreme Council of the Association of Planets! In the year to come, the people of Earth will begin trading their abundance of extra food for advanced technological instruments and devices, which will have the immediate effect of expanding food-producing capabilities of every country on this planet. This will increase the rate of food production exponentially. Once the people of Earth have successfully demonstrated their continuing peaceful intent, all of the technological secrets of the Association of Planets will be yours for the asking. Interstellar space flight, methods of propulsion for traveling faster than the speed of light, will be revealed to you. Their fantastic technology advancing the critical concepts of not merely extending life but enhancing the quality of your life will also be shared. Good people of Earth, there are a myriad of other potential benefits of living, traveling, and being that are waiting to unfold themselves unto you as a result of this alliance. But it is up to you, the people of Earth, to be ready to accept them. These promises, I am afraid, must come with a warning. There can be no compromise of conscience. If the people of Earth fail to proceed along the path of peaceful existence, if you fail to follow the Association of Planets guidelines and regulations toward a new peaceful and prosperous Earth, then you will find yourselves embroiled in a mindless dance of catastrophe, destruction, and utter annihilation. There can be no more chances given. There will be no more warnings. People of Earth can no longer act with relative impunity. From the depths of space, planet Earth will be disintegrated. No form of life on Earth will survive. Not one. This is a fate and punishment too horrible to contemplate. I beg of you, please do not let that happen."

I could readily discern a noticeable, horrified gasp echoing throughout the crowd. I paused a moment to emphasize my point. As I looked at some anxious faces among those assembled, I could see the effect my words had on them. Their minds were alert and receptive, and for the first time in a long time, I felt a sense of hope for the people of Earth. After a moment's silence, I finished my address . . . my exhortation to the world's listeners.

"As for myself, Klaatu, and his daughter, Moori, have offered me the singular kindness of an invitation to make their planet my new home. I have accepted. I have found love with a beautiful and kind woman, and we plan to start a family. I am told I will probably live to be at least one hundred and fifty years old there, all due to the different atmospheric conditions, along with their advanced science and technology. Furthermore, this is a planet that has laws but very few, if any, lawyers. Next to being a member of the government, a lawyer is one of the lowest professions one can aspire to here. Also, the ruling government on planet Muurae, which is kept as small as possible, exists solely for the good of the people, unlike Earth-type governments of the past, which were self-serving and promoted only their own existence. Here, the government truly serves the people, not, as it was on Earth . . . the people existing to serve the government. There are no illegal taxes on this planet. People get to keep what they earn, and the government has no right to take anything that they have not earned. There is no stupidity or ignorance here, for they have learned to live without it. That means war does not exist in their part of the galaxy, either. I pray that one day, with the help of the Association of Planets, this will be the case with the Earth as well. We have been quite successful in implementing the correct form of government on Earth. It is, as always, now up to you to remain vigilant against possible usurpers of the people's powers. Guard the form of government we have established . . . with your very lives. For your very lives depend upon it.

Well, the time has now come for me to leave you. I present you with this narrative, with this description of what happened, how, and why it happened. I consider it essential that the people of Earth learn from the profound knowledge that has been presented and accept the peaceful way of life being offered.

It is my sincere hope the mistakes of the past, which have caused immense catastrophe and destruction, are not repeated. Not only do all of my thoughts and prayers of good fortune and prosperity go out to each and every one of you, but those of Klaatu and the Association of Planets do as well. For my wife, Moori, and, for myself, I say . . . good-bye and good luck, and may the Almighty Spirit guide you in your decisions, and bless you . . . always."

Made in the USA
Monee, IL
15 September 2021

78106901R00169